"*DEAR GOD, give me strength and courage to meet each day with a high heart and unswerving devotion...*"

With this prayer, lovely young Jill Ordway entered on her duties at Kimberly Sanitorium.

Jill's first months at Kimberly had been filled with the joys of a hard job well done. Shoulder to shoulder with Dr. Kim she worked to make his dream of a haven of comfort and healing come true. But now a storm was gathering—a storm which was to sweep the girl into its vortex of fear and hatred.

Lucy Agnes Hancock's novels of the nursing profession are read and loved by millions of women. GRADUATE NURSE is her unforgettable story of a young girl's courage and loyalty.

# GRADUATE NURSE

*Originally published under the title*
**DR. KIM**

*by Lucy Agnes Hancock*

**WILDSIDE PRESS**

# GRADUATE NURSE

THE DEEP SHADOWS of a wet October evening gave the rather overpowering drawing room of the Webster mansion on River Boulevard a subdued and soothing atmosphere. Only one small lamp, near a sofa at one end of the long room, was lighted and there was no sound except for the crackling of the fire in the huge grate. The sole occupant stood immobile— his back to the blaze, his face unnaturally somber in so young and virile a man. Once he slowly lifted his right arm and stared at the hand, flexing the fingers experimentally, then allowed it to drop to his side. He didn't hear Wilkins enter until the butler spoke.

"A cocktail, sir?" he asked, presenting the tray to the young man. Then, "You're looking very fit, Doctor."

"Thanks, Wilkins," the man answered, accepting the drink.

"Miss Sylvia sent word she was unavoidably delayed, Doctor," Wilkins explained. "She was sorry and hoped you would understand. Is there anything else, sir?"

"That will be all, thank you," Bruce Kimberly said, wishing now that he had taken the time to call his sister instead of rushing away from Medical Center in order not to keep Sylvia waiting. He sighed, walked to a window and turned as the butler left the room. He stared at the glass in his hand for a moment then returned to the fire and set it on a corner of the crowded mantel. He loathed the Webster concoctions and, anyway, Sylvia knew he wasn't supposed to touch the stuff—especially just now. He resumed his position in front of the blaze. He wondered what was keeping Sylvia. Seven-thirty. Mr. Webster breezed in and slapped Bruce on the shoulder, elaborately particular to make it his left shoulder.

"Sylvia's late again, I see," he said jovially. "These women! They drive us crazy with their dilly-dallying and yet we wouldn't be without them, eh, Doctor?" He took a cocktail, disposed of it in one or two gulps then came to stand beside Bruce, his hands behind his broad back. Bruce fidgeted. "How's the arm, boy?" Mr. Webster asked.

"About the same," the young man answered, making no move to demonstrate.

"Oh, give it time, give it time," Sylvia's father said tactlessly. "Anyway, I wouldn't worry too much. After all, the world is full of surgeons—good ones, too. Of course we realize you're disappointed; but you're young—surgery isn't the only field open to you. You can have a desk in my office any time you say the word. There's still money to be made in the market, you know. Now, now, it was just a suggestion," as Bruce turned to glare at the big man beside him. "The trouble with you returned servicemen is nerves. Relax, boy—relax. The world is still a pretty good place. You can still play a good game of bridge—even get in some golf later on, perhaps, and if you insist you can no doubt hand out pills and prescriptions with the best of them. I tell you, you've got a lot to be thankful for—a lot to look forward to."

Bruce felt a tightening of his nerves—felt his left hand clench, then he sighed deeply and let go. He was a fool to mind anything the old duffer said.

Horace Webster went on: "Why don't you come down to Florida with us next month, Bruce? You need a change—of scene—conditions—people. Great place, Florida—great climate—make a new man of you—fine people down there— some of the best. How about it?"

Bruce shook his head. A sudden and unreasonable rage filled him. What did this smug, overstuffed millionaire know of him —what he needed? He had always rather liked Sylvia's father but just now he felt that he hated him. He took a step forward —he wanted to get out of the house—away from this stupid heckling. And then Sylvia came into the room and ran to him.

"Darling, darling, I'm so upset," she cried, rubbing her cheek against his shoulder. "That horrible Lowell creature talked on and on for simply hours and I couldn't just get up and walk out on her. Kate would never have forgiven me. What were you and Papa talking about?" She traced a frown on Bruce's forehead with one slim finger. "I bet I know. He doesn't approve of that sanatorium idea either, do you, Papa?"

"Never mentioned any sanatorium, my dear," her father said. "Didn't think it worth mentioning. No person in his right mind would dream of tying himself to anything of the sort. No money in such a scheme—no money at all—but plenty of headaches. Don't worry about Bruce. He and I have plans—the boy's nobody's fool. He knows on which side his bread is buttered. Eh, son?" His elbow dug into the young doctor's side and Bruce winced but not from pain.

Fortunately, dinner was announced and Mrs. Webster, resplendent in black lace and diamonds, joined them. The meal wasn't particularly festive, however, and Bruce was relieved when it was over and the older folk departed for the theater. Sylvia drew Bruce into the library and settled herself on the arm of his chair.

"What's the matter, lamb?" she cooed. "Something go wrong with your plans? Tell Sylvia, darling." Her voice was soothing, gentle, adoring and the young man relaxed, his head against her shoulder.

"I'm still edgy," he apologized. "I don't know what I can expect from these new X-rays but—well—it will do one of two things—give me hope or prove that surgery is definitely out as far as I am concerned." He raised his right hand again and examined the fingers with something like resentment. Sylvia's arm pressed him close.

"Don't you care, darling," she whispered. "I'll love you just the same no matter what they prove. You shouldn't be so sensitive, Bruce. Be thankful it doesn't show. Honestly, one would never suspect you of being a cripple—O-oh, I'm sorry. I didn't mean to hurt your feelings," as he made a startled movement and drew back from her embrace. "But you will have to get used to it, my dear. It's quite honorable, you know, and I'm terribly proud of you."

"So you think of me as a cripple?" he asked morosely.

"Of course not," the girl said quickly. "You're my splendid Bruce and I love you. Why can't you come down to Florida with us next month? We could have such wonderful times—swimming, sailing, fishing and—oh, dancing—lots of dancing."

Bruce caught her close even while he shook his head. "Nothing doing, sweetheart," he told her. "I may be a cripple, but I am still capable of earning a living for myself and family—if any. I think the negotiations for Lakeview Sanatorium are going through all right, and——"

The girl drew back. "But, darling, you aren't fit to work yet. How can you even think of such a thing? Later, perhaps, but

3

not now. You need relaxation, fun, lots of sunshine—you should get away from this beastly climate——"

Bruce grinned up at her. "You forget I'm a working man, my love," he said. "Why, even your father thinks I'm still able to hand out pills and prescriptions."

"Oh, Papa!" the girl said impatiently. "What does he know about it? But honestly, I think you should get away from the winter—the cold and ice."

"Nonsense! I love winter—skating, skiing, ice-boating. I'm a product of the north."

After a long moment the girl said firmly, "Then I shall stay, too. I shall refuse to go South with the family." She waited for his appreciation of her sacrifice and snuggled against his side. "We'll have fun, won't we, Bruce? You won't bury yourself in that old sanatorium so that I shall never see you, will you? I love you, darling," she murmured against his cheek.

The telephone on the desk whirred and she picked it up. Her expression changed as she said coldly, "Yes, he is here. Who is calling? Oh, it's you, Ruth. Just a minute." She held the instrument out to the young man and said impatiently, "Your sister, darling. Don't let her take you away."

Bruce grinned at her. "Hello, Ruth!" he said into the transmitter. "What's on your mind? What? Who? No! Well, well, Jill Ordway? Are you sure? Where did she call from? O-oh! I can't right now. Okay. See you later."

He replaced the instrument and stared into space for a long moment, his thoughts chaotic. He hadn't seen Jill Ordway since leaving the hospital in Tunis. So she was back in America. A grand girl. He hoped to see her—soon—very soon.

"Well?" Sylvia asked, her voice tight. "And who may Jill Ordway be, my dear Bruce? Another of your devoted nurses? And what does she want of you, anyway?"

"Want of me?" Bruce murmured, his thoughts miles away. "Want of me? Why—nothing."

"Then why does she telephone you—or your sister—at this hour? It's after ten. Who is she and what is she to you?"

Bruce laughed and with his left hand cupped the lovely round chin of his fiancée and looked deeply into the long-lashed blue eyes, just now dark with resentment.

4

"Jealous?" he teased.

Sylvia drew away. "You haven't answered me. Is she the nurse who wrote our letters—the one who read to you—did all the amusing things you told me about and later picked out the souvenirs you brought home? Oh, I knew all along you never chose those trinkets. A woman did that and I suppose it was this paragon Jill—what a silly name!"

Bruce still continued to smile. "Don't be a goose, Sylvia," he said at last. "Jill knows all about you. She listened to my ravings about your beauty—your sweetness and my luck in winning you. She thinks you're the loveliest girl she ever saw —from your picture. Why, Jill's a pal—a girl in a million. The boys adored her."

"I can imagine; but I bet she's in love with you."

"Nonsense!" the man answered sharply.

"Why can't we be married, Bruce? I mean now—this fall, and not wait until spring or until you're able to practice again? I have enough for both——" She laughed angrily. "I never thought I should reach the point of begging a man to marry me, but, darling—why should we wait longer? It isn't helping any."

Bruce drew away and walked to stand before the glowing fire. "We threshed all this over before, Sylvia," he said quietly. "This sanatorium will take every cent I can lay my hands on. I've got to do it my own way, darling—without help from anyone. Can't you understand, dear? I have my pride. I wish you didn't have a penny—and we could build our future together. No, Miss Webster, there will be no wedding until I have made good—until I can support a wife in something of the style to which she has become accustomed." He was smiling as he finished speaking and the girl frowned, then suddenly laughed lightly.

"You're a silly, hidebound, puritanical despot, Bruce Kimberly, but I adore you," she said coming to stand close, her head against his shoulder. "It shall be just as you say, you big bully, and I shall stay right here in Westhaven all winter. I hope you appreciate the sacrifice and if I get pneumonia I shall insist on coming to your sanatorium so that you can take care of me."

"It's a deal," the young man said, his arms about her, his

5

dark head against her bright hair. They stood so for several minutes until the girl murmured, "I wish Ruth hadn't called you, Bruce. Why was it so important?"

"Oh, I don't know. I suppose she wanted me to know that Jill was in town. You see, I made her promise to look me up when she got back to the States. She's a darned good nurse and I can certainly use a few good nurses out at Lakeview."

"Was she at your apartment, Bruce? Did Ruth——"

"Ruth is at the sanatorium—has been for a week or more. She will manage it for me until I can get squared away."

"Then how did this Jill get in touch with her?" Sylvia persisted.

"Probably Ruth came into town for something and—Oh, I don't know. What does it matter? I hope you're not going to develop into the sort of doctor's wife who resents his women patients and his nurses. If you do, you're letting yourself in for some most unhappy times."

"And I hope you won't become the sort of doctor who thinks only and always of his patients—and nurses—never of his wife. I'm sorry, darling. I guess I'm just jittery tonight. I'm so crazy about you that I resent your interest in everyone but me. Don't scold, Bruce. I'm sorry and I promise to be good."

"That's my girl. Now I've got to run. I promised to—see a dog about a man," he said grinning down at her. "Jeff Thomas has a brainful of bright ideas he wants to discuss with me tonight and I told him I'd meet him at ten-thirty sharp." His kiss was warm and Sylvia relaxed in his arms. She was reluctant to let him go; but he drew back at last and moved to the door.

"Have lunch with me tomorrow, darling?" she asked as he shrugged into his raincoat. "I'll meet you at one—at the Chatham Grill. Can do?"

Bruce shook his head dubiously. "I doubt if I can make it, Sylvia," he told her. "I'm going to have a pretty full day. I'll try, only don't wait for me."

Sylvia pouted for a minute and he stared at her in bewilderment. She smiled and patted his arm. "Don't mind me, lamb," she said soothingly. "I've had a hectic day and I'm tired. Run along and see your dog about the man—or——" She stopped and patted his arm again. "Phone me when you can spare a minute."

They kissed again and Bruce let himself out into the wet October night. It had stopped raining but a cold wind was blowing from the north and he pulled his scarf more snugly about his throat, then with a gesture of impatience shrugged it loose again. Between Ruth and Jill he was becoming a molly-coddle. Jill! So she was in town. He certainly wanted to see her. Ruth had sounded quite excited. He wondered if they had met and what she thought of the nurse who had done so much for him during those long, dark, hopeless days in Tunis. His heart warmed at the memory. He hoped Jill would come to the sanatorium with him—she had promised to do so. In fact, her enthusiasm about the project had been the deciding factor that had made him investigate Lakeview Sanatorium—had given him hope and vision for the future. It was good to know she was back—actually in Westhaven. He would look her up first thing in the morning. Bless her!

He stepped out briskly. Things were looking up. Perhaps the X-rays would hold out a tiny bit of hope.

2

BRUCE KIMBERLY was in anything but a happy frame of mind when he left Westhaven Medical Center next morning. Maybe it was childish of him to have anticipated a miracle—dreamed that the latest X-rays would show any marked improvement. He knew that physically and mentally he was as well as ever —that his sojourn in Bramton Sanatorium had done all that the eminent Doctor Havelock had promised; but it was apparent that his arm and hand still remained impaired. He knew definitely now that as a surgeon he was washed up. Just why he had supposed conditions should have changed in the three months he had been away, he didn't know. Perhaps it was due to the fact that for the first time since that piece of shrapnel had found its mark in his right forearm—the subsequent infection with its nightmare of fear for his hand and the slow, galling inactivity ending in the nervous collapse—he felt perfectly

7

well. He now knew the worst. His career as a surgeon was over.

He recalled Sylvia's somewhat tactless comments to the effect that he was by no means licked. That no one would ever know he was a cripple—that it didn't show too much. He could move his arm and hand—still a trifle stiffly to be sure, but they were useful and would doubtless become more pliant as time went on. She had reminded him that he could still dance— still play a keen game of bridge and be as charming as ever— when he could foregt his lost career.

"And, darling," she had confessed, snuggling against him, "now we can be married at once and I shall have you to myself. No more being put off with the excuse of hospital work. No more broken dinner dates, theaters, dances and trips because some patient was thoughtless enough to demand immediate attention. No, my darling, I can't feel too terrible about this calamity. Of course I was proud of you as a successful young surgeon, but there have been times when I was most dreadfully jealous of that career of yours."

And he had said nothing, knowing full well how disappointed he must often have been to her—the girl he had asked to be his wife. It was simply that she didn't understand. He sighed as he recalled that first day of his return from overseas—blue and discouraged, sore in body and soul, that he had broached the idea of giving her up—releasing her from an engagement that no longer held the glowing promise of a brilliant future. She had been hurt. She had come to the hospital to see him—welcome him back, and had leaned close to him, raising wide, tragic blue eyes to his sober face, making him feel a veritable heel. He had actually drawn back from her clinging hands—drawn away from his lovely girl—his dream girl. He sighed impatiently and shook his head as if to rid himself of the memory.

"She should have ditched me then and there," he told himself. "But why can't she see my side of it? She should know me well enough to realize I could never consent to live on her money—be a kept man." He shuddered at the picture. Then had followed months in the sanatorium—months of discouragement and black despair and his slow—painfully slow recovery.

Doctor Havelock had suggested he remain at Bramton as

Assistant Chief of Staff and when he had demurred had mentioned the smaller, somewhat exclusive sanatorium a couple of miles south of Westhaven.

"What it needs is young blood, Doctor," the old man had said. "It has slipped rather badly these past few years. However, it has splendid possibilities—wonderful location—good buildings and once had a better than average staff, except for the fact that most of it is like the hospital—hidebound. The war, however, played havoc with it as with all of us. Why don't you look the situation over, my boy?"

"Just what's the matter with it?" he demanded cagily. "You say it has slipped——"

"Oh, it is, or was, a corporation—a lot of old fuddy-duddies put their money into it a couple of generations back and little or nothing has been changed since. It's hard to get young, modern nurses and doctors interested in it because it's sort of isolated, but that could quite easily be remedied these days, or made to be an asset under proper management. I have a notion old Doc Morgan will listen to any reasonable proposition you may offer. Doc's the biggest stockholder—practically owner. I'll back you if you like. I think you could make something pretty wonderful out of Lakeview."

Sylvia hadn't liked the idea at all. She foresaw the curtailment of even the brief time Bruce could give her. They had had their first real quarrel over the sanatorium situation, but in this instance Bruce was firm. His sister, on the other hand, was enthusiastic and after paying a visit to Lakeview fell completely under its spell. So, after a thorough investigation, the proposition looked far too good to pass up. He proceeded to make arrangements to take over the management and Ruth moved in as superintendent, replacing elderly Mrs. Arnold, a rotund, talkative little woman only too glad to shift responsibility and retire to her own home in town.

Jeff Thomas was keen to join him as technician. They had been in medical school together and Jeff had done some excellent research work. The small laboratory at Lakeview, while by no means up-to-date, held exciting possibilities and the young man was enthusiastic. What if the place showed neglect inside and out? Together he and Bruce could revolutionize Lakeview so that the sanatorium would became famous. And while they were about it, why not get hold of Pete Allison for

9

some snappy advertising? Bruce had laughed at the other's eagerness and now, as he was striding along in the wet October morning, he smiled involuntarily at the memory and turned abruptly when someone called his name.

"Doctor Kimberly! Oh, Kim—wait a minute!"

A tall, hatless girl in a white raincoat was running across the street quite unmindful of traffic. Bruce stepped to the curb and held out both hands. He completely forgot his disability.

"Jill! Jill Ordway! I was coming to see you—if I could find out where you are staying." His hands were warm and close on hers. They stood so for a long moment oblivious of the few passers-by who stared, smiled sympathetically and went on their way.

"Oh, Kim, you look wonderful!" the girl said. "I'm so glad!" Her voice proved it and somehow the young doctor felt strangely heartened.

"And *you're* not exactly hard on the eyes," he grinned. Then drawing her hand through his arm he said, "Let's go somewhere and talk our heads off, Jill. I have so much to tell you—so much to listen to—here, let's go in here. It's almost noon—we'll have lunch." He stopped, then went on, "Sylvia is meeting me here at one. I want you two to know each other, Jill."

"But that's more than an hour away, Kim," Jill demurred.

"What of it? But—where are you parked? Hotel?"

"No, I'm staying at the Y. W. for the time being. We could go there. It isn't far and then you could meet Sylvia at one and I could go on about my business."

"Let's see—there is a cafeteria connected with the Y. W.?" the man asked.

"Of course. But I had a late breakfast—unless you're hungry. You always used to be, didn't you?"

"Sure I'm hungry. Let's go—if it's open."

It was and they collected their various items for lunch and found a table in a far corner of the big room. Over coffee and hot roast beef sandwiches, they relived their days in the service. Bruce told of his hospitalization in this country and Jill recounted her experiences in Sicily, then Italy, France and finally in England.

10

"And how about your sanatorium, Kim?" she asked as she ate a generous wedge of apple pie. "Have you done anything about it? Your sister seemed to think it was your child and it was up to you to introduce it. And how is the hand— I'm sorry if you're sensitive about it, but you don't need to be that way with me, you know. In fact, I think you need not answer. I knew as soon as you shook hands, but I guess I knew even before that—in Tunis. Now tell me about the sanatorium."

"It's all sewed up, Jill. Ruth's already established there and I expect to take over before the end of the year. Coming in with me? You said you would, remember? It's a lovely spot —trees—splendid trees, hills and a lake within walking distance. Good buildings and fair equipment, and I think I can promise you some interesting cases. There's a nurses' home— on the grounds. It's not too far from civilization—only a couple of miles from here. Care to visit it? We could go out there any time you say."

"I'd love to go, Kim." She glanced at her watch. "It's quarter of one. I think it's time you started for your luncheon date."

"I wish you would come with me, Jill. I know Sylvia wants to meet you. She appreciated your letters and all the stuff you bought for me to bring home."

But the girl shook her head. "Not today, Kim. Some other time. I, too, want to meet your lovely fiancée. I hope she will like me."

"Of course she will. She'll be crazy about you—can't help it."

As he shrugged into his raincoat he didn't hear Jill's murmured, "I wonder."

But she wouldn't have wondered long if she could have been present at the small table in the Chatham Grill a few minutes later. Sylvia Webster toyed with her salad, broke a French roll into tiny pieces and sipped the black coffee almost absently. She ate practically nothing. Bruce urged her to at least drink the coffee but she shook her head.

"I'm neither hungry nor thirsty," she said. "You're not eating much yourself," she pointed out.

Without thinking the young man said, "I lunched an hour ago."

11

Sylvia stiffened. "You did? When you were meeting me for lunch?"

Bruce flushed. He was on the defensive. "It's a good thing I did, considering the farce you are making of yours," he laughed.

"Where did you lunch?" she asked.

"Well, I'll tell you," he said deliberately. "I ran into a friend of mine I hadn't seen in some time and we went to a cafeteria and talked our heads off."

"I see," Sylvia murmured, then abruptly, "So, Jill Ordway found you. I thought she would."

"Found me? Nothing of the sort. We ran into each other on Foster Street when I was coming from the Center. Gosh, but it was good to see her again. She's a grand girl. I'm anxious to have you two meet. I want you to be friends."

"Just what is she doing in Westhaven, Bruce? Does she live here? If she does I never knew it."

Bruce shook his head. "No, Jill's from the Middle West—Michigan, I believe. At least she has a brother out there—an engineer. Her parents are dead. This brother brought her up. She's crazy to meet you."

"H'm'm—I doubt it," Sylvia retorted skeptically. "You haven't answered my question. What is she doing here? Followed you, didn't she?"

"Don't be ridiculous, Sylvia. Of course she didn't follow me. I made her promise to look me up when she returned to the States. She's a swell nurse and I can use a few good nurses out at Lakeview. Don't be catty, sweet. I want you two to be friends."

"We'll see," Sylvia said and changed the subject to one nearer her immediate plans. "The Winslows are having a house party at their summer place this next week-end, darling, and I have accepted for us both. We are to leave on Friday afternoon and drive over. It's only about a hundred miles or a little better—nearly all State road. Two other couples—all good friends of yours—are going, too. It should be lots of fun and don't you dare refuse or I shall be really angry." She paused to light a cigarette. "Tony Miller will take their station wagon, so all we have to do is relax and enjoy the scenery—and each other."

A long sigh escaped the man opposite. He shook his head.

"I wish you wouldn't make plans for me, Sylvia," he said. "There are a thousand things I have to consider just now. Can't you realize that, darling?"

The girl frowned. "I realize that you don't seem to consider your own health," she said smoothly. "You are in no condition to burden yourself with work or worry. I don't know what that sister of yours is thinking of to let you even consider going to work yet or for a long time to come. Well, I'm not going to let you—I'm going to take care of you. It's very evident that neither you nor anyone else will. You need relaxation and fun and you're going to have them. Understand?"

She was very pretty in her concern and Bruce's eyes told her so. He pressed the hand near his on the table and whispered, "I see I'm going to become a much pampered husband—one of these days."

"Do you mind?" she asked through lowered lashes.

"What do you think?" he asked.

"Then you'll come? I'm so glad," Sylvia said happily. "Neal and Addie Winslow have a lovely place—huge, with private beach, golf and tennis—stables and a big productive farm. They're sweet—both of them—and they have three adorable children. You'll love it all."

"But I scarcely know the Winslows, Sylvia."

"Oh, they admire you a lot, darling," Sylvia told him. "They know all about your heroism—the decorations you received and your injuries and they're crazy to have you with them. Don't worry—they have heard so much about you they probably consider you one of them."

"How did they hear?" He gazed narrowly at the girl opposite. "What I did was nothing compared to all that our nurses experienced. They were the real heroes of that ghastly night." He shuddered at the still poignant memory.

"You mean Jill Ordway, of course," Sylvia said coldly.

"Jill was one of them. They were all splendid. You remember, don't you, that three girls lost their lives? It was a miracle any of us survived." He spoke quickly—his tone one of reproof.

Sylvia said nothing for a moment, then with eyes filled with tears she whispered, "I'm a beast—a nasty little cat, Bruce. How can you bear the sight of me? What can I do to show your Jill that I am grateful for helping bring you back to me?"

13

"Just be sweet to her, darling," the young man said contritely. "She admires you no end and you can do a great deal for her. You see, my dear, she is all alone here. I imagine I'm the only person in Westhaven—in this part of the country probably—she knows. It must be very lonely for her. Just be your own sweet self, Sylvia. I shall ask nothing more."

"I hope the weather will be good over the week-end, Bruce," Sylvia murmured to change the subject, "Addie and Neal are anxious to see you." She laughed demurely. "I guess I've done a lot of boasting about you, darling. Do you mind—terribly?"

Bruce grinned a bit shamefacedly. "I suppose it was to be expected—under the circumstances," he said resignedly. "But I'm afraid I shall prove something of a disappointment in the role you've given me. I'm not the stuff from which heroes are made, I fear. However, I shall endeavor to wear the laurels you have forced me to wear as gracefully as possible. The best I can hope for is that your pals will excuse the deception—putting it down to the rose-colored glasses through which you view me and my record. Love's a wonderful thing, you know, and quite capable of turning the drabbest, most commonplace of lovers into a veritable Lochinvar."

"You're far too modest, Bruce Kimberly," the girl chided.

"Have it your own way," he retorted resignedly. "I'm as putty in your hands—and you know it."

Sylvia Webster's eyes were very bright—her smile beatific as they left the place. Bruce could be difficult on occasion, but she knew how to handle him.

3

It was the next morning that Sylvia Webster, in smart black suit and furs, stopped her blue roadster at the curb in front of Westhaven's Y. W. C. A. She was in anything but an amiable frame of mind. Bruce had been late in arriving the night before and then had seemed unusually absent-minded. Pete Allison and his mother had dropped in and the two young men had been continually reminding each other of their war experiences—of friends met or lost—of scenes grand or horrible, until Sylvia had exclaimed in exasperation and demanded the conversation be brought into pleasanter channels.

Pete, who had known her since childhood, grinned and said teasingly, "Okay by me, Syl," and settled back in his chair to ask reminiscently, "Whatever happened to that pretty nurse the men in your division were so keen about, Doc? They called her Jill, I remember. Someone told me she was transferred to another unit after you left, fella. Some gal! I never saw her but once. We ran into each other in a hole-in-the-wall on the filthy outskirts of Tunis. A slimy rascal was haggling over the price of a certain scarf she wanted. Well"—he grinned and eyed Bruce knowingly—"she got the scarf. Ever hear from her, Doc?"

Before Bruce could answer, Sylvia said sharply, "Oh, she's here in town. Didn't you know? She followed Bruce to Westhaven, Pete. That's devotion for you—or isn't it?"

"Gosh, Syl!" Pete cried in mock distress. "Don't tell me you're jealous—of a mere nurse—and planning to marry a doctor. Heaven help you, woman! To think of you—Sylvia Webtser—jealous! Now I have seen everything!"

"Don't be an ass!" Bruce exclaimed irritably. "Miss Ordway is going to work out at the sanatorium. She's a darned good nurse and, believe me, we shall need a few good nurses. Sylvia is just trying to be amusing."

Sylvia said nothing for a moment and Pete Allison eyed her through half-closed lids. Beautiful, of course, but there was a feline quality there he had never noticed before. His mother rose to leave and Bruce mentioned a date with Jeff Thomas, which Sylvia felt sure was made on the spur of the moment, and all three had departed together. It had been a most unsatisfactory evening.

She recalled all this as she glanced in the mirror and patted a curl in place. After a moment she got out and walked up the short brick walk to the big front door. She opened it and went in. A gray-haired woman in a blue tailored suit and crisp white blouse smiled at the newcomer's momentary hesitation and said cordially: "Good morning! May I help you?"

"Thank you," Sylvia said coolly. "I'm looking for a Miss Ordway who is supposed to be staying here. I wonder if I could see her?"

"Just a moment," the woman said, feeling chilled and re-

15

senting it. "I will see if she is in her room. Won't you be seated?"

But Sylvia preferred to remain standing while the woman pressed a buzzer and a maid appeared and departed. In a moment or two she returned with the information that Miss Ordway was in her room and would see the visitor. It was the room at the end of the corridor on the third floor. She watched the tall, beautiful blonde mount the stairs and disappear, then turned to Mrs. Clarke and whispered, "Do you know who that is, Mis' Clarke?"

Mrs. Clarke, a newcomer in Westhaven, shook her head. Her manner said quite definitely that she neither knew nor cared particularly.

"That's Miss Webster—Sylvia Webster. Ain't she somethin' though?"

"She most certainly is," Mrs. Clarke smiled and Hetty, the maid, went back to her work.

Upstairs in the room at the end of the corridor, Jill Ordway stood waiting. She wondered who her caller might be. She hoped it would be Ruth Kimberly, Bruce's sister. She turned at the knock on her door.

"Come," she said cordially and went to greet the stranger.

"Good morning," Sylvia said coolly. "You're Miss Ordway? The nurse?" She hadn't offered to shake hands and Jill caught hers back, holding it firmly as she answered, "Yes. I am Jill Ordway, R. N. And you?" although she thought she knew. Suddenly she felt antagonistic toward the beautiful young woman in her sumptuous furs and expensive hat.

"Don't you know?" Sylvia inquired haughtily. "I understood from Bruce that you had seen my picture——"

"Oh," Jill exclaimed as if seeing the light for the first time, "of course. You are Miss Webster—Kim's fiancée. Won't you sit down? I was just going out but I can wait. It is kind of you to look me up, Miss Webster."

"Bruce has told me about you—how you nursed him during his hospitalization in Tunis; did all sorts of amusing things to bolster his morale—although I confess I'm skeptical as to the necessity for such diligent attention. You see, I happen to know that Bruce is and always has been a very sane, level-headed person. But I suppose an attractive young doctor must expect to endure a great deal of maudlin sentimentality from

16

the nurses associated with him. I wasn't fooled in the least, Miss Ordway. And that impossible junk he brought home with him—I had an idea he never bought all that atrocious stuff. Bruce has such exquisite taste! I wonder just where you unearthed it."

Jill laughed, forcibly quelling her anger. "The shops and stalls in Tunis are simply fascinating, Miss Webster," she said, her voice nostalgic. "One buys and buys, scarcely realizing just how trashy some of it is until you get it away from its environs. I'm sorry you don't care for it, but it was fun buying it, anyway. Doctor Kimberly and I had a lot of fun looking it over." She added that last almost defiantly.

"It doesn't matter," Sylvia said indifferently, "I am wondering how you happened to pick Westhaven—why you decided to come here, Miss Ordway," she said.

Jill stiffened. She knew that Sylvia Webster was trying to hurt her and her head went up proudly.

"I came because I promised Doctor Kimberly to come to him when I returned home. I am planning on working in his sanatorium. I hope you have no objection, Miss Webster."

Sylvia laughed derisively. "Don't be silly. Why on earth should I object? Bruce needs nurses and he thinks you are an excellent nurse. I was just interested—curious, if you like— as to just why you followed him here."

"Well," Jill answered coldly, "now you know."

"Yes. Now I know," Sylvia said, her voice tight. "Well, I doubt if it will do you much good, Miss Ordway, for I think the sanatorium idea won't last long. Bruce knows I don't approve and—well, after all——" She turned toward the door, which was partly open. A trio of young women were loitering outside. They were grinning roguishly and Jill flushed in annoyance.

"Good-bye, Miss Webster," she said coldly. "So kind of you to look me up and—don't worry about me—or Kim." She said the last more to herself than to her caller and when the door had closed between them she grinned wryly and reached for her coat. But the door had opened a bare crack and a bright head came through the aperture.

"Who's your ritzy friend, Jill?" the newcomer asked. "Now don't tell me. Let me guess. One of the upper crust—slumming, no doubt. Dear, dear, what us woiking goils have to

17

endure! Just what was biting her, sweetheart?" she wanted to know. "She looked at me as if I were a worm. H'm'm—the back o' me hand to her."

Jill shook her head. "Search me," she retorted.

"Isn't she the gal who's engaged to Doc Kimberly, Jill?"

Jill nodded. "Beautiful, isn't she? And what furs! Wow!"

"I don't think she's so wonderful," Ann Burke said, wrinkling her pert nose. "Looks sort of dressed up—artificial. I bet she's a cat. Doc had better watch his step with that one. Going downtown, Jill? I'd walk you over as far as Doc Ford's. Hope I'm not late for my appointment. It's something of a major victory to get a dental appointment these days."

The two girls left the building and walked the short mile to the business district. Jill told herself she didn't care what Sylvia Webster thought of her; but she was suddenly depressed. She had come to Westhaven with such high hopes. She and Bruce Kimberly had been through a lot together. She had nursed him during those terrible weeks when there were fears of losing his entire arm. How she had fought to save it! There had been days and nights with death all around them when she had knelt beside his hospital cot while delirium rode him, whispering encouragement, praying for him, singing softly his favorite songs, while the roar of battle ebbed and flowed in an endless tide. She had helped prepare him for his journey back to the United States, swallowing her fears and fighting tears of homesickness as the great plane bore him aloft—carrying him away from her care. She had received two letters from him—one written by his sister, the other picked out on a typewriter by Bruce himself. The sanatorium they had planned together when he lay discouraged and sleepless in the hot African night was materializing at last. She must come to him. He needed her. It was a brief letter, but priceless to Jill Ordway.

Jill had not yet met Ruth Kimberly, but she liked her already. That first night when she had called the Kimberly apartment, the voice answering her was pleasant—even friendly—and after Jill had made herself known, Bruce's sister had been warmly enthusiastic. She had wanted to meet the girl who had done so much for her beloved brother but she was due at the sanatorium, in fact the car was already at the door. But she wanted to see Jill as soon as possible. When could she come

18

over to Lakeview? Was she ready to go to work at once? Jill shrugged away the memory of Sylvia Webster's visit. Perhaps it was natural that she should resent anyone else being close to Bruce—caring for him—doing the things she hadn't been there to do. And yet, Jill felt it was more than that with Sylvia. She sighed deeply. Kim was such a grand person! He deserved the best and she felt somehow that Sylvia Webster was not the one for him.

She wandered about the city after Ann left her, stopping at shop windows to stare unseeing at the lavish display of fall hats or coats or frocks. She didn't know why she kept on walking. She felt restless, uncertain. Perhaps she should leave at once for Lakeview and get to work. She turned and retraced her steps. She would go to the bus terminal and find out about transportation. She already knew there were no train accommodations. The ticket agent told her there was an early morning bus leaving at six-thirty. She hesitated a moment, then bought a one-way ticket. She would go back to her room and pack. As she entered the hall of the Y. W., Mrs. Clarke called to her.

"I have a telephone message for you, Miss Ordway," she said, handing her a slip on which she had written a number. "You were to call that number as soon as you came in."

Jill went into the telephone booth and dialed the number. A man answered and asked her to wait. In a minute a voice said, "This is Sylvia Webster, Miss Ordway. I wonder if you would care to come in for cocktails this afternoon—and, of course, tea if you prefer."

"I'm sorry," Jill replied stiffly. "I'm afraid it will be quite impossible. I am leaving town tomorrow and shall be very busy."

"Leaving town?" Sylvia turned and spoke softly to someone in the room and then said, "I'm so sorry. Bruce is anxious for us to meet—to become friends, you see, and——" She hesitated, then asked sweetly, "Would you mind telling me where you are going, Miss Ordway?"

"Why, not at all," Jill said evenly. "I'm going out to Lakeview Sanatorium."

"To Lakeview—but—— Oh! Well, if you aren't leaving until tomorrow you can still come here this afternoon. Shall I send the car around at four, Miss Ordway?"

19

"No," Jill said emphatically. "That won't be necessary, for you see——"

"I'm so glad," Sylvia interrupted. "I'm looking forward to meeting you," and before Jill could protest further, the connection was broken.

Now, she asked herself, what brought that on? Why didn't she invite me this morning? And why act as if we hadn't already met? Bruce was probably right there beside her while she was telephoning. That must be the explanation. She didn't want to go. Sylvia made it quite clear she had no desire or intention to be friends.

"I won't go," she said aloud and went on upstairs. She packed the few things she had taken from her bags during her three days' stay in Westhaven and went down to the cafeteria for lunch. She was hungry and filled her tray with an assortment of appetizing food, found a table from which she could view the room and sat down to enjoy the meal. The room filled rapidly and she found the diners interesting to watch. So many girls—office girls, she thought, and boys from the Junior College. A few older men and women, but for the most part the people there were young. The food was good and she was thoroughly enjoying it. Her thoughts wandered.

"May I sit here?" someone asked, and Jill was startled.

"Why—why yes, of course," she said and the tall young man set his tray on the table across from her.

"I hope you don't mind," he said somewhat diffidently, and Jill saw that he looked almost apologetic. "I dislike eating alone," he explained.

"That's perfectly all right," Jill told him cordially. "I'm used to it."

"Does one ever get used to it?" he asked, putting butter on a bit of roll.

"Oh, yes," Jill said. "In fact, I think one can get used to anything—in time."

She was nearly finished and the young man said, "I wish you wouldn't hurry. It's good to have someone I know sitting opposite. Do you live here? And would you mind telling me what you do—for a living, I mean? I think I could guess——"

There was nothing in the least fresh or objectionable in

20

this young man's manner and Jill smiled. "All right," she said, "guess."

"I think you're either a teacher or a nurse."

"Why?" she demanded.

"You are self-reliant. You have poise and that certain air of knowing what you want and feeling sure you are going to have it."

There was a twinkle in his eye and he spoke softly but with conviction.

"Are you by any chance a seer—a crystal-gazer?" Jill asked, laughing.

"Why? Am I right and which are you? A nurse, I think."

"Right. I am a nurse," Jill told him. "Now let *me* do a bit of crystal gazing. I think you are an instructor or perhaps a minister—something to do with books. You have the look of a seeker after truth."

"Wrong!" he said triumphantly. "You're way off. I'm a scientist—a technician—a searcher after truth, perhaps, so maybe you're not too far off the beam. My name is Jefferson Thomas, B.S., M.D., very much at your service." He crammed his remaining piece of pie into his mouth and lifted his cup.

"Don't eat so fast," Jill warned, "or you'll be searching for bicarbonate of soda. I'm Jill Ordway and I have lived here just three days and am leaving tomorrow morning for Lakeview Sanatorium where I have the promise of a job. What's the matter?" For the young man had risen and held out both hands to her.

"Oh, happy day! At last I've met you! Lucky me! So you're the gal who brought Bruce Kimberly back from death's door intact and set him on the road to life, liberty and the pursuit of—Sylvia Webster's idea of happiness. I'm—gosh, I'm glad to know you! When do you leave for Lakeview? I'm going up there on an early bus—tomorrow."

"Six-thirty?" Jill asked, finishing her coffee. She was glad. She liked this exuberant young man—this stranger who suddenly seemed like an old friend.

"What are you doing this afternoon?" he asked, making a ball of his napkin.

"We-ll," Jill began, "I have a sort of half-date for cocktails —or tea, as Miss Webster informed me—at the Webster mansion, but——"

21

"Don't," the young man protested. Then, apologetically, "Do you know Sylvia—Miss Webster, Jill? I shall call you Jill —if I may. It just suits you. I wish I had been named Jack instead of Jeff, but do the best you can with it—please!"

"I've met her," Jill answered guardedly.

"That should be enough. I've met her and it was more than enough—for me. But then I'm such a barbarian—such a plebeian, you know. Tell me, did it ever strike you that Bruce is a bit off—er—balmy? What can he see in that blonde hussy? Tell me."

Jill laughed wryly. "Well, she's beautiful—she's rich—she belongs to the elite—she can do a lot for Kim——"

"You don't think that's it, do you?"

"No, I don't," Jill replied honestly. "I think he loves her— madly. I think he would love her if she hadn't a cent and worked for a living. Kim's that sort."

Jeff Thomas stared at the girl opposite for a long disconcerting moment and then whistled softly. "Well," he said at last, "I guess you're right. It must be love——"

Jill got to her feet. "I shall probably see you again, Doctor Thomas—Jeff," she said, smiling at him.

He caught her hand. "But you haven't told me what you intend to do with this afternoon. Why can't we spend it together? There's a pretty good picture at the Criterion, or would you prefer just doing the town—having me point out the items of interest like the reservoir, the Webster mausoleum, the Medical Center where I have been a more or less valued employee, the three rather good parks just now being tucked in for the winter, the Junior College up on the hill and, oh, Westhaven is no slouch of a town at that."

"But the Webster affair—the tea?" Jill demurred. "I suppose I should go."

"Okay. Let's both go. If she looks too surprised to see me, I'll tell her we have a date—important date for dinner too and I came to see you didn't stay too long. I know those cocktail fights. Crowds—people milling about bumping into each other —drinking a lot of the vile stuff called the Webster Specialty— and stuffing thin sandwiches and sickly cakes. The tea must be something new—or is it old? One never knows what the glamorous Sylvia has up her sleeve. We'll just drop in for a minute or two and drop out again—none the worse for the experience

22

—I hope. You'll save your reputation and I'll save your life. Okay?"

Jill laughed. "Okay," she agreed. "I think I should enjoy the grand tour—if you don't mind. Do we walk?"

"We do not. I know a chap who owns a car. I'll borrow it and we'll go in style and comfort. My bus is still in hock—so to speak."

And that's what they did—roaming far and wide—and they reached the Webster mansion soon after four. Jill, who had relieved her tweed suit with a white frilly blouse and a small green velour hat with a provocative orange cockade—an outfit that had come straight from a tiny but exclusive shop in London, brought a whistle of admiration from her new friend when she joined him. The tea or cocktail hour was as Jeff Thomas had predicted—a crush. Wilkins greeted Jeff as if he recognized him, though none too cordially, and ushered them into the drawing room where Mrs. Webster was serving tea while her daughter, looking ravishing in a stunning creation that must have cost plenty—went from group to group and back to the tall young man who stood back to the glowing grate —his gaze on the door. So it was that the first person Jill saw when she entered was Bruce Kimberly, and as their eyes met across the crowded room, her heart warmed. Suddenly she no longer cared what Sylvia Webster thought, said or did. Bruce was her friend and life was good. Doctor Kimberly came forward and caught her two hands, staring in surprise at the young man beside her.

"I didn't know you two knew each other," he said.

"Oh, there are lots of things you don't know, my lad," Jeff told him airily, his hand on Jill's arm. "Jill's looking well, isn't she? And are we going to have fun tonight!"

Bruce looked annoyed for a moment and drew Jill with him to meet Sylvia. "I want you two to be friends," he said, and Jill was astonished and puzzled that Sylvia made no mention of their having met before. She wondered why but felt that it wasn't worth bothering about. Sylvia chatted animatedly for a moment, a possessive hand on Bruce's arm, and Jill had a strange feeling that perhaps she had dreamed that unpleasant visit to her room at the Y. W. The girl was sweet and friendly —her smile cordial, and Jill became increasingly bewildered. Sylvia's greeting of Jeff Thomas was on the surface courteous enough, although Jill detected an undercurrent of aversion—antagonism, as if Sylvia wanted to put him in his place. Jeff, however, remained quite at ease.

Suddenly she turned to him and said coolly, "I understood you had left town, Doctor Thomas. But I'm sure any of Bruce's friends are most welcome—can feel free to drop in at any time."

Bruce beamed at his love and Jeff pinched Jill's arm. He grinned imperturbably and bowed deeply. "So good of you," he murmured. "But we aren't staying long. Jill and I have a heavy date—our last free, untrammeled night in dear old Westhaven."

"How nice for Miss Ordway," Sylvia said, while Bruce gazed from one to the other, a puzzled frown on his face.

"Nicer for Jeff Thomas," that young man pointed out and drew Jill, who had said practically nothing since her arrival, toward the door. Bruce would have followed but his fiancée's touch became firm and she said sharply, "Wait, Bruce!"

He looked at her in astonishment. People were milling about, apparently oblivious of the drama being played. The street door closed and Bruce asked, "What is this? I don't understand."

"You wouldn't," Sylvia answered. "What sort of a girl is this Ordway person, Bruce? I invite her here because you insisted we become friends, and what does she do? Scarcely opens her mouth—remains five minutes and leaves. Has she no breeding—no social experience? I'm afraid your taste in friends is proving a bit questionable since the war, my love. Jill Ordway —Jeff Thomas!" Her voice held scorn and Bruce flared to their defence.

"They may not belong to your set," he said sharply, "but I would stake my life on the goodness and integrity of either of those two. They are among my very best friends and as such are welcome wherever I am. Remember that." He stalked away and Sylvia bit her lip in annoyance.

"Well," her mother pointed out, "what can you expect? I warned you how it would be if you persisted in your mad infatuation, my dear. Really, it would have been better had you listened to me and taken Peter Allison. At least he is one of us."

Sylvia turned on her mother and said softly—almost menacingly, "Don't worry about Bruce, Mama," she told her. "He'll

24

learn, darling—how he'll learn!" She smiled but without humor.

Her mother shrugged slim shoulders. "I wouldn't be too sure, my dear," she murmured warningly.

4

"Do you intend running a neuropsychiatric hospital, Bruce?" Sylvia Webster asked her fiancé on Friday morning as they waited for the Miller station wagon to appear. She shuddered. "You're morbid, darling. Why can't you forget the war and what it has done to people and take life as you find it? I can't see the necessity of spoiling our future by deliberately taking on the troubles of others—complete strangers. You're far from well yourself, so——"

"We have been all over this before, Sylvia," the young man pointed out, "and you will have to let me do as I think best. As far as conducting a sanatorium for neurotics—well, there will undoubtedly be many of such in need of the treatment that we can give them at The Kimberly Sanatorium—which, by the way, is to be our new name. But we expect to treat the physically ill as well as those suffering from mental illness."

"But you will, no doubt, treat more of the latter. It will be a sort of lunatic asylum," the girl said, her lip curling. "A nice, happy future you have planned for yourself—and me."

Bruce shook his head, his dark eyes sombre. "No. No, my dear. No actively insane people. However, there are a great many neurotics who simply need the proper care to bring them back to a normal state. In fact, almost everyone suffers from a neurosis of some sort—at times." He smiled down at her, his arm about her yielding shoulders. "One of yours seems to be—at present—an antipathy for my chosen career; but no doubt you will recover—completely—in time."

Sylvia drew away. She looked into his face and said seriously, "This is no joke to me, Bruce. While, of course, you must do as you think best, I doubt if I shall ever be entirely reconciled. You see, it is all so unnecessary—out of character. Why, you have changed already. Just contemplating this sanitarium—well, sanatorium, then—has aged and sobered you. Oh, I know you

25

blame it on the war, but it isn't all due to that. It's your morbid interest in the ailments of a lot of derelicts——"

"I guess you will never understand," Bruce interrupted sadly, turning away.

With a little cry of protest, Sylvia flung herself into his arms. "I'm sorry, darling. Please don't be mad at me. I worry so about you—why won't you listen to me—for a while—until you're well again?"

She was so lovely—fair head against his breast, face uplifted, blue eyes pleading, that his irritation evaporated. His arms tightened about her and he held her close for a long, satisfying moment. The sound of a musical horn outside in the driveway made them draw reluctantly apart.

"There's Tony and the gang," Sylvia said happily. "Let's go. Oh, this is going to be such fun!"

Together they went down the steps of the ornate stone porch to be greeted by four rather noisy young people, out for a good time. This was Sylvia's idea of life, Bruce thought morosely, and made an effort to snap out of his somber mood. Perhaps he had let his tragic disappointment darken his outlook on life. Maybe he did need rousing, getting away from everything and anything that reminded him of the war. It could be that Sylvia was right and he was morbid—had taken himself too seriously. Well, he owed it to the lovely girl beside him to forget the past and his altered plans for the future and enjoy with her these few carefree days.

He had never particularly cared for any of the quartette that for the next couple of hours were to be closely associated with him on the drive to the Winslow summer cottage. He grinned wryly to himself as he thought of that cottage with its forty rooms and two dozen baths, its huge ballroom, its outdoor pavilion with swimming pool, its famous golf links, its stretch of private beach. "Cottage," he muttered mockingly, and colored guiltily when Sylvia turned to him happily and asked, "Comfortable, darling? Isn't it splendid the weather man decided to give us a good day? It's warm as June."

"Anyone who wants to take a turn at the wheel is welcome," Tony Miller said over his shoulder as they left Westhaven behind and sped along the broad highway. "How about you, Greg? I don't suppose the gals or Doc would oblige a feller?"

"Of course not, you big bluff!" his wife laughed. "You

know you adore this monstrosity and wouldn't let one of us lay a finger on that wheel."

"Let me drive, Tony," Sylvia suggested, grinning at the others. "I'll just call your bluff, pal."

"Oh, I wouldn't think of separating you two lovebirds," Tony jeered, passing a huge truck by a narrow margin, and increasing speed.

Bruce, who enjoyed driving, bit his lips. He had little sympathy for speeders and longed to tell this smart young man that it would be well to slow down to the regulation fifty miles an hour and avoid the danger of accident; but he saw that none of the others seemed concerned and he remained silent, calling himself an old granny for worrying.

The ride was without incident except for several narrow escapes, and they arrived at the Winslow estate with unabated enthusiasm. Neal and Addie Winslow, surrounded by some half dozen dogs, were on the front terrace and greeted them with apparent delight. The exuberant welcome of the dogs produced varied results from the new arrivals—squeals of protest from two of the girls and expressions of approval from the men. Bruce, especially, met the animals as only a dog-lover could and they seemed to sense his friendship, for they frisked about him, leaping to his outstretched left hand and barking joyously. Sylvia watched him with mounting excitement. Perhaps this was the answer. Perhaps this was the way to circumvent the insidious infatuation for a career tied to a sanatorium. She made a mental note to visit a near-by kennel as soon as she returned to Westhaven.

"It's such a lovely, warm morning that breakfast will be served on the back terrace. The lake is on its good behavior," Addie Winslow said. "I was so afraid we were to miss out on Indian summer this year—the weather has been more like November than October. Do any of you want to freshen up first or will you come out right now? Backus will see to your things."

"Gosh, Addie," Tony Miller growled, "I'm simply filthy. Which suite are we to have, old gal? I'm shedding this dusty outfit and getting into fresh clothes before I so much as look at food. How about you, Doc? Although you and the rest had it pretty soft coming up here."

Mrs. Winslow touched a bell and a slim young girl appeared.

"Please take Mr. and Mrs. Miller to the blue suite, Beulah," she told her, then turning to Bruce she said, "I'm sure you will enjoy rooms facing Ontario, Doctor, so I'm putting you in my favorite rooms in the bachelor wing. You are to be up this way, my dear," she told Sylvia, "and you and Greg will have your old rooms at the end, facing the front terrace, Marie. We have had them done over since you were here last year. I hope you like them."

Upstairs in the elaborate rooms—called part of the bachelor wing—Bruce Kimberly thought what a wonderful sanatorium could be made of this huge summer home. But he supposed money couldn't buy it. The Winslows were enormously wealthy; but they were nice people. He liked them better than the majority of Sylvia's friends. For one thing, they were older and like most real aristocrats they were kindly folk—gentle and considerate in their dealings with their fellows. Neal Winslow had been a pilot during the war and carried his injured leg with scarcely a limp. The Winslow children were nowhere in sight and Bruce wondered if they were here at all. But after he had changed into lighter clothing, he wandered down the long hall and descended to the main floor where through wide-open windows came sounds of shouts and laughter. He followed the sounds and came upon two sturdy boys, seven and nine, and a girl of perhaps five, romping with the dogs. He stood and watched until, spotting him, the dogs rushed upon him. He held out his left hand to meet their onslaught and the children shouted their approval.

Then the older boy, noting the guarding of the man's right hand and arm, asked, "Were you in the war, sir? Was your right arm injured? Will you tell us about it, please?"

"Now, Larry, dear," his mother, who had approached, remonstrated. "Doctor Kimberly wants to forget all that just as Daddy does. Run along to the other side, darlings, and take the dogs with you like good chilluns. We'll be going for a swim in a little while. Scoot!" She turned to Bruce and apologized. "I'm sorry, Doctor," she said.

"I don't mind talking about it, Mrs. Winslow," the young man told her, "except that—well—it wrote period to my chosen career. But we all paid a price for victory—some more —some less."

28

"I know," the woman murmured sympathetically. "Neal feels the same way. He feels his price was low compared to what some were compelled to pay. Tell me about your plans, Doctor. I heard something about your taking over a hospital or sanatorium. How does Sylvia like that idea?"

At the sudden darkening of the young man's eyes she said quickly, "I was sure of it. She doesn't like it, does she? Well, I shouldn't feel too discouraged about it. She should feel proud of you—proud of your resourcefulness—your ability to adjust yourself to altered conditions. Some men can't, you know. Oh, here you are." She turned to Sylvia, who came at once to stand beside the young doctor—to slip her hand through his arm possessively. "I've been getting better acquainted with your doctor, my dear," she said graciously. "I think you are a fortunate girl."

"Aren't I, though?" Sylvia smiled, her adoring eyes on Bruce's face.

"Break it up, you two," Tony Miller jeered. "We've all been bitten by the love-bug in our day and recovered—thank Heaven! Did you say something about food, Addie?" he asked, grinning at his hostess and patting the heads of the only two unmarried ones in the party. "Bless you, my children, and all that, but come on now—let's eat. Where's Neal, by the way?"

"Gone to look at a sick colt. He'll be back directly," Neal's wife said, leading the way around the thick shrubbery to where, on a broad terrace in full view of the placid, sparkling Ontario, an attractive meal was set. Neal Winslow appeared almost at once and the meal proceeded with much laughter and good-natured ribbing back and forth. Sylvia and Bruce endured the usual amount of teasing and the girl noted with satisfaction that Bruce took it all with ease and amiability.

"What's the matter with the colt, Neal?" Greg Howard asked during a lull in the conversation. "Anything serious? Don't forget we have a doctor in our midst, old man. Perhaps he can prescribe." His tone was light.

"Bruce is an M.D., Greg, not a vet," Sylvia said sharply.

"So what?" the young man retorted. "Disease is disease whether in man or beast. M.D., Doctor of Medicine. Right, Doc?"

Bruce nodded. "To some extent, Howard," he agreed. "If I

29

can be of service I shall be very glad," he added, turning to his host.

"Maybe I shall take you up on that, Doctor," Neal Winslow told him. "You see, our local vet is a busy man and since he entered politics last year he has sort of neglected his veterinary duties. He promised to drop in during the day, and Mike, my stable men, says he'll keep after him until he gets here."

Sylvia was annoyed. She was afraid of this new development. Why couldn't Greg Howard mind his own business? She knew that Bruce would be only too happy—right in his element—offering suggestions, helping with the care and treatment of anything sick—horse or man. And after the meal, their host and Bruce went along to the stables and nothing was seen of them until midafternoon. At last, Mrs. Winslow called the stables and was told that the colt was responding to treatment and she could look for them very soon; but lunch was over and the guests, with the exception of Sylvia Webster, were on the links when the absentees returned. They were tired and somewhat soiled but jubilant. As they approached the house Neal Winslow slapped his guest on the back.

"Great work, brother!" he said, and catching sight of his wife, who had left her seat to meet them, he explained jovially, "Doc here beats any vet I've ever had, Addie. I've just offered him a permanent job as local animal doctor at these diggings. I bet, at that, he'd make more dough than he will at that sanatorium he's heading."

"Money doesn't mean a thing to Bruce," Sylvia said, an edge on her voice. She had been keeping her hostess company and was feeling very much abused. "Papa and I have tried to talk him out of his mad scheme but like most men he's stubborn. He won't listen to us."

"Good for Kimberly!" Neal applauded. "Nothing like a streak of stubbornness, my boy. Stick to it after you're married—don't be wife-ridden. Be a man—not a mouse, I always say, don't I, darling?"

"Do you?" his wife asked demurely and there was a general laugh that cleared the air. "Run upstairs and get rid of that stable odor, you two, and your lunch will be served out here with Sylvia and me. Perhaps we'll even keep you company—at least with a drink."

Bruce hummed as he bathed and changed into fresh gar-

30

ments and was surprised to realize that he felt better than he had in days. He liked these Winslows. They were genuine. He had always been fond of horses and as a youngster on his doctor father's farm had often helped treat the local animals for minor ailments. He was glad to have been of service today. He knew that Sylvia was annoyed at his absence but, after all, there had been nothing else for him to do. She must realize that. He hung his coat across the back of a chair near a window and stared dubiously at his shoes that were smudged. He turned as a knock sounded on his door, and at his "Come," Backus entered.

"I came for your suit and shoes, Doctor," he said. "Ah, here they are. I'll have them back to you in an hour." From the door he turned to say, "Splendid job you did on the colt, sir. We are all very happy about it."

"Why—why, thank you, Backus," Bruce replied, somewhat touched by the man's evident pleasure. "I was glad to be of service."

"That's what makes it so splendid, sir," Backus said. The door closed and Bruce was puzzled for a moment as to just what the butler meant.

It was something less than an hour, however, when Backus returned with the cleaned and pressed suit and snowy shoes.

"Here you are, sir," he said. "Something else I can do for you, Doctor?"

"Thank you, Backus—you were very quick. I think I can manage nicely—now," Bruce told him.

"Thank you, sir," Backus said and departed. Bruce grinned to himself. Service with a smile—sincere service. That seemed to be the slogan of the Winslow menage.

He went downstairs and found Sylvia alone on the wide terrace. She watched his approach with a smile of contentment. This was the life for them. Some day they would have just such a place—perhaps not so large at first, but something of this sort, and he would keep busy and contented taking care of an occasional sick animal—or one of the servants. She, herself, was never sick. There would be no need of his working—having a practice—being at the beck and call of a lot of silly, neurotic women. They would have such a good life— long seasons spent at their country estate—winters in Florida with flying visits to New York for the theater or shopping.

31

She sighed blissfully and held out a hand to the tall young man.

"Happy, darling?" he asked, slipping to the grass beside her chair and drawing the hand to his lips. "Lovely place, isn't it?"

"Ours will be just as nice, Bruce," she told him, "except that we shall have the great Atlantic at our door instead of a mere inland lake. It's lovely up there. You'll love it."

"You mean your father's place in Maine? But——"

"One can dream, can't one?" the girl asked hastily, her golden head turned up toward the soft October sky, her eyes musing. "Dreams are so comforting—while one is waiting, darling."

Bruce said nothing for a moment and Neal and Addie Winslow found them so—hand in hand gazing off into the distance. The two watched for a long moment and Addie slipped her hand into that of her husband and he smiled down at her understandingly.

"Beautiful, aren't they?" she whispered. "Contrasts."

"Yes," he agreed quietly, "in more ways than one, I'm afraid."

His wife nodded but said nothing more as the maids appeared with food and cold drinks.

Back in the Kimberly Sanatorium, Jill Ordway was adapting herself to the somewhat limited conditions in which she found herself. Ruth Kimberly was all the girl had anticipated and Ruth, in her turn, felt that in this strangely appealing girl was the answer to many of her vexing problems. Together, she confidently believed, they could reorganize the nursing staff to make it something splendid. Bruce had enthused to her about Jill's ability as a nurse—her efficiency, fearlessness, sound common sense; but he had not mentioned her sweetness, beauty or selflessness.

"Blind—blind—blind!" Bruce's sister said of her absent brother. "Why are men so blind? Why will they chase after a phantom—an hallucination—and fail to see or appreciate the lovely truth in plain sight?" She sighed, then shook her head. "Ruth Kimberly," she chided, "mind your own business. Hands off—though perhaps an occasional little nudge in the right direction might not be amiss."

## 5

JILL MISSED MANY things at the Kimberly Sanatorium that were part of a general hospital. She missed attending operations, of which there were none except the simplest or minor sort. But she discovered she had a distinct aptitude for nursing neurotics and was thankful for her long months of training in a psychiatric hospital. And while most of the cases here were, as yet, mild, there were one or two returned veterans who required and received her constant and devoted care. Ruth Kimberly, delighted with this girl, began to see the fulfillment of her earlier dreams of a staff composed of supernurses—nurses who spared not themselves—who cared only that the patient recover and worked toward that end.

"I wish we had a dozen like her, Bruce," she told her brother as they were discussing the slow but encouraging improvement in the condition of young Tim Woodworth, a returned flyer. "She seems to be endowed with a sixth sense. The patients adore her and she can make them do just about anything she suggests." Miss Kimberly sighed. She was tired. "We have not enough *good* nurses, Bruce. That Ann Burke you mentioned won't be here for another week and we need her badly. Already we have several applications for rooms. But there, I shouldn't burden you with these problems. Forget it, dear. We'll manage."

"I knew you would like Jill, Ruth," her brother said. "But you should not expect to find all nurses as good as she is. She's quite exceptional, you know."

"No," his sister denied. "I don't think so. A well-trained nurse should be good at her job. A Training School—if it is a reputable one—sees to that. I have a mind to send you to one or two of which I know and see whom you can interest in our particular project. I'm sure Julia Anderson, over at Wimble Memorial, will help. They are graduating a small class next month and I know that every graduate is good. Why not run over there and see what you can find?"

"Why not go yourself, Ruth?" Doctor Kimberly demurred.

33

His sister smiled. "Ah, but I'm merely a woman, my dear —a nurse to be sure, but still a woman," she chided. "Now, you're a man—and an attractive doctor—oh, yes, you are, Bruce, and I'll wager you'll return with—oh, maybe half a dozen names—two or three of which will give us at least a trial. Why not plan on going tomorrow—Wednesday."

Bruce Kimberly frowned. "Must it be tomorrow, Ruth?"

"Why not?"

"Oh, Sylvia has made plans for tomorrow, but——"

Ruth Kimberly bit her lip. "I suppose you might make it Thursday, then; only the sooner we get things organized here the better. We certainly can't accept more patients until we do, you know."

Bruce got to his feet. "I'll call Sylvia at once," he said firmly. "She should know better than to make plans for me. I've warned her against it repeatedly, but—well—you know how impulsive she is, Ruth."

Ruth nodded, her lips compressed, her mild brown eyes cool. How well she knew the impulsiveness of Sylvia Webster —only she gave it another name—plain, unadulterated selfishness. However, she said nothing and listened to the one-sided conversation with increasing misgivings. How long would Bruce be able to hold out against the insidious maneuverings of his beautiful but utterly spoiled fiancée? She heard her brother's voice change—become cool, and she relaxed; but then it changed again—he was pleading, coaxing, chiding—and at last to Ruth's annoyance she heard him say resignedly, "Okay, sweetheart. You win."

Ruth Kimberly stiffened. So Sylvia had won again. But she gave no sign of her disappointment. "So it will be Thursday, then," she said. "Jill and I can certainly use some efficient help." She purposely inserted Jill Ordway's name, realizing her brother's admiration for the nurse. Bruce swung about.

"The girl is entitled to some consideration," he cried, his voice harassed. "After all, we are engaged and I have been able to give her precious little of my time during the past four years."

"Of course," his sister agreed amiably. "I don't blame her in the least for wanting you with her. You see, I do myself." She laughed and patted his hand. "Don't worry, my dear. Jill and I will manage—somehow."

34

"There you go," the young man muttered. "And don't think I'm not aware of our dire need here and believe me, my bossy sister, I'm taking over next week instead of next month, whether you like it or not." He strode from the room and his sister shook her head ruefully.

"Darn Sylvia Webster!" she muttered as she followed her brother from the room. She heard the outer door close and knew Bruce was on his way to the house which they were to occupy just as soon as the present chief-of-staff and his wife should vacate it. She hoped it would be soon, as she felt sure that with her brother under her supervision he would have less time to devote to the demanding and possessive Sylvia. She was confident that his beautiful blonde fiancée was not helping in his recovery. He might be better off right here getting used to the place. She knew he wanted to wait until Doctor Morgan should leave but perhaps she could hurry that along. She felt sure the old man was eager to be rid of the place and was only staying because she had felt Bruce shouldn't be rushed. Now, however, she wasn't so sure. Perhaps Bruce needed some small shoving—to gradually shoulder a bit of responsibility.

She mounted the stairs and began her morning visits—the tour of inspection that kept her abreast of conditions. She had an idea that some of the nurses—two in particular—resented her; but neither one was especially efficient and she felt no least twinge of regret to know they would be leaving very soon. It was better so. Changes in management invariably brought changes in the personnel. It was to be expected. She had heard the nurses grumbling over the rules and restrictions she had instituted. They had done as they pleased for so long they didn't take kindly to any curtailment of what they considered their rights. Well, the Kimberly Sanatorium was going to be managed properly and those who didn't approve or were not willing to co-operate could leave. She had her own ideas and was confident of ultimate success.

The first room she entered was occupied by one of Westhaven's wealthiest though most eccentric female residents. She was Mrs. P. Hamilton Botany, sixty-eight, widowed and possessor of several millions. Ruth greeted the scrawny, bitter-faced woman with a friendly, "Good morning! And it is a very good morning—our first real Indian Summer day if we are to believe the radio commentators. How are you feeling, Mrs. Botany?"

"Terrible!" the patient replied shortly. "But very much as usual. I have a grievance, Miss Kimberly. I want to know why I cannot have Miss Ordway as special instead of the poor stick assigned to me and whom I sent packing just before you came in. I simply cannot stand the creature. I am paying top prices —old Morgan saw to that—the miserable old Scrooge. I have been practically keeping this place going for years and he knows it and I should have a few privileges. I will have you know that I have influence—a great deal of influence—and have the power to make or break a place such as this. Well?" she asked. "What are you going to do about it, Miss Kimberly?"

Ruth Kimberly smiled into the sallow, unhappy face of the patient and said evenly, "Let me tell you a little about the problems facing us right now, Mrs. Botany. Miss Ordway is already doing the work of three nurses and I'm sure you have no desire to add to her already heavy burden. We are expecting several new nurses within a few days or weeks and I'm sure everything will work out satisfactorily. You have the best rooms in the place, my dear, and I have personally been watching your diet so that your meals were nourishing and appetizing. I'm sure Miss Ordway would like nothing better than to have the exclusive care of you, Mrs. Botany. I believe she admires you, you know. But you realize how things are just now. Doctor Kimberly is taking over the management next week instead of next month as planned. He is anxious to get back to work. I'm sure you will like my brother, Mrs. Botany, for you see, I am very fond of him." She laughed gently and watched for an answering gleam in the clouded eyes opposite.

But Mrs. Botany wasn't to be amused easily. She eyed the superintendent narrowly for a long moment but Ruth Kimberly stood her ground without flinching. "Well," she said at last, "if what you say is true and the Ordway girl admires me —though I have a feeling you're something of a pleasant liar, my dear—I can assure you the admiration is mutual." Her sigh was gusty, however, as she went on: "Busy as she is, don't you think she might, perhaps, spare me a few minutes occasionally? I'm not an unreasonable woman. I couldn't have stood what I have all these years if I were. I shall demand little

36

of her; but the girl is like a breath of fresh air—a stimulating draught—an incentive to live. Who is she, Miss Kimberly? What do you know about her—her people—her background?"

The superintendent shook her head. "I know that she is a graduate nurse and that she served twenty-two months overseas in the Nurses' Corps where she met and nursed my brother, Doctor Kimberly, in a hospital in North Africa. She is an orphan, I believe, having been brought up by an only older brother who lives somewhere in the Middle West. She is twenty-five years old and unencumbered, I understand. Does that answer your questions, Mrs. Botany? Her name is really 'Juliet' but she hates it."

"I like that girl, Miss Kimberly. She reminds me of my own youth—when I, too, faced the future with enthusiasm and plenty of hardihood. But I lost both that eagerness and fearlessness long ago. I have no future—nothing to look forward to—except death."

"Nonsense!" Miss Kimberly said robustly. "You are by no means an old woman. There is nothing really wrong with you —physically. You have wealth and you say yourself that you have influence, so you have a splendid future—to use both for the good of others and"—she added to herself rather than to the patient—"for the good of your own soul."

"H'm'ph!" snorted Mrs. Botany. "I've been coming to this place for years and this is the first time I have known Lakeview Sanatorium to go in for preaching."

"We have changed our name now, Mrs. Botany," Ruth told her, smiling. "Hereafter we shall be known from coast to coast as The Kimberly Sanatorium."

"H'm. Coast to coast, eh. Ambitious."

"I have no doubts whatever but we shall become quite famous—in time." She laughed at the woman's stare of almost shocked incredulity. "We, my brother and I, believe in hitching our wagon to a star. By aiming high we shall certainly reach a greater elevation than if we made our target the nearest blackberry bush. Don't you agree?"

"I suppose you expect to get rich—overnight," the patient scoffed.

"Rich? You mean make money?" Ruth shook her head vigorously. "Indeed we do not. What we hope and pray for is the chance to help people—the worried, the mentally ill, the poor harassed victims of our mad and unhealthy civilization, the war casualties who have failed to become adjusted to civilian life; and believe me, Mrs. Botany, there are more of them than any of us realize."

"How old are you, Miss Kimberly?" the sharp-eyed patient demanded.

Ruth laughed and shook her head. "Now that is a question no woman so close to thirty likes to answer. Why do you ask?"

"Close to thirty? Nonsense; you're still an adolescent with stars in your eyes and froth in your head. Not expect to make money indeed. Bosh! Everyone expects—or at least hopes— to make money. What else is worth striving for?"

"Stick around, my dear lady," Ruth told her, "and you'll see."

"I shall," the patient assured her firmly. "Perhaps I shall find it interesting."

"I'm sure you will." The superintendent laughed and turned to leave the room. But Mrs. Botany wanted the last word and had it.

"It's about time I got some entertainment for my money," she said, and the door closed on her rasping chuckle.

Tim Woodworth in room 47 had been suffering from a psychosis traceable to his months in a concentration camp hospital. His case was particularly pathetic due to the fact that his fiancée—an English nurse—had been killed during the bombing of London and his only and adored sister had been lost at sea early in the war. When he came to the Sanatorium some months before, his case had appeared practically hopeless. Diagnosed as involutional melancholia, he was watched closely to prevent suicide. There had been talk of releasing him to a State institution for the insane, but the trustees managing his parents' estate wanted him to remain where he was for further treatment. It was only since the advent of the Kimberlys that he had shown the least sign of improvement. He had fallen a prompt victim to Ruth Kimberly's charm and clung to her presence whenever she came to his room, mutely pleading for her understanding. The superintendent used to watch his efforts to express himself—his restlessness—his constant reaching for imaginary objects—his maneuvering to obtain paper, pencil or even a towel or washcloth which he would

38

tie into knots or carefully pleat and as carefully press smooth again—his need for something with which to keep busy—something to occupy his mind and hands. And Ruth, who was a firm believer in occupational therapy where at all possible, decided to put a plan into practice.

"Did you ever try weaving, Tim?" she asked one day as she stood beside his bed. "It's fascinating. I have a small, light frame that I shall be glad to lend you and will show you how to use it. You could quite easily make scarves, neckties and even small table mats. Do you think you might enjoy using it?"

The hopeless, almost vacant blue eyes gazed at her for a long wordless moment before he shook his head. "No use," he muttered huskily. "Die—must die—no use——"

"Indeed it is some use, Tim," Miss Kimberly assured him, breaking into his broken, almost hysterical wail. "And you are, too. I hope to move into Doctor Morgan's house soon and I could use several items you could make for me—if you care to. I need a scarf for my hall and innumerable table mats. They are easy to make and pleasant to handle and you might even find a market for them when you become really proficient," she explained, carefully ignoring the fact that Tim Woodworth was well endowed with this world's goods and had no need of earning money. "Bruce—Doctor Kimberly—brought back some really fine pieces of weaving when he returned from abroad, Tim. I'll lend them to you so you can get an idea of the possibilities there are in that small frame. Are you game to try?"

Her tone was so friendly—so sane and matter-of-fact, that Tim Woodworth became interested in spite of himself and his discouragements.

"Okay," he said, and Ruth's heart lifted. From that day on, the ex-flyer showed marked and steady improvement, and on the day he finished his first slightly irregular and nondescript table mat which he dubbed, with unexpected humor, a dishcloth—his recovery was assured. Soon there was not a nurse in the place who didn't own one of Tim's gay and colorful scarfs, nor a male inmate, whether doctor or patient, without one of his neckties. Even the two yard men proudly displayed vivid neckties, and he worked so rapidly that very soon Ruth Kimberly possessed such an array of woven items that she was at a loss for places to use them.

"I shall take a few into Westhaven and see if perhaps there is a market for Tim's weaving," Ruth told her brother the day they moved into the brick house. "He has really done wonders."

"But with all the Woodworth money there is no need for him to earn more, Ruth," Bruce said. "After all, it has served its purpose—carried him over the bridge. That's all we hoped for."

"I wish there were someone belonging to him. It seems to me that is all he needs right now. Have you found out anything more about him, Bruce?"

"No one very near," her brother replied. "Jill discovered that he used to live in a little village upstate—oh, several years ago—when he was just a youngster. He told her about some neighbors of his family, and a boy and girl he used to play with. He spoke almost nostalgically, Jill said, and she wondered if perhaps that might not be the answer."

"It might be," Ruth agreed. "I'll find out about it and try to get in touch with them. If he could go there—visit these neighbors for a while, it might complete the cure. Oh, I hope so, Bruce. He's such a nice boy. He wouldn't be able to go for a Thanksgiving but we might engineer a Christmas invitation for him there. Here, help me with these curtains, dear. I lack your inches if not your brains."

Bruce gave her a playful shove and hung the curtains while his sister stood back and observed the results. The house was beginning to look like home to these two who had spent much time apart. They looked forward to a happy life together and Ruth hoped it would be unending with no Sylvia Webster to mar the intimate and affectionate relationship.

6

DOCTOR KIMBERLY'S VISIT to Wimble had netted the sanatorium three nurses. Thanksgiving was just around the corner and on this sunny, blustery November day he was in excellent spirits. He felt he had a great deal for which to be thankful. Pete Allison was doing a great job of advertising. Jeff Thomas had the laboratory in excellent shape and was already showing results. Workmen had succeeded in restoring the battered and long unused left wing and, at a cost much below the owners' estimate, had given the sanatorium five extra rooms, all of which were already spoken for. He ran up the steps of the main building and into the wide hall, feeling himself able to cope with any emergency that might arise. His sister was descending the stairs, a sheaf of papers under one arm.

"Hello!" he greeted her. "It's cold outside. Nice, though. Makes one glad to be alive. I saw Morley and he will operate first thing in the morning—if he agrees with my diagnosis, and I'm certain he will. Now all we have to do is obtain Mrs. Fowler's consent." He opened the door to his office and paused to let her precede him. "Anything happen while I was gone?"

Ruth shrugged. "Nothing much, except a visit from Sylvia."

"Sylvia! What did she want?" Suddenly his high mood seemed to slump.

"I took her on a tour of inspection, Bruce," Ruth told him. "I'm afraid she doesn't have a very high opinion of our sanatorium. I don't know what she expected, but it was quite definitely not what she found. She isn't at all reconciled——"

"Reconciled?" Bruce interrupted sharply. "Why should she be? Why is it necessary that she should be? It's my work—my business—my career. She knows that because I have explained it to her time and time again. So she wasn't pleased?" His gaze wandered about the shabby office—once Doctor Morgan's and now his—and back to his sister's serene face. He sighed deeply. "I can see her side of it, Ruth," he said ruefully. "Her parents have quite thoroughly spoiled her. She has always had too much money and too much leisure——"

"My dear Bruce," his sister interrupted in her turn. "Sylvia Webster is no longer a child. She's a woman. She's intelligent enough—or should be—to realize that she can't dominate every situation. After all, how long do you suppose her love for you would last if you yielded to her wishes to give up your career and live on her money? Become a social butterfly—a kept man? No. No, my dear brother, the only way you can keep her respect and affection, if any, is to stick to your guns—be independent—a man, not a mouse." Her face was flushed with earnestness and her brother nodded.

"I agree with you, Ruth," he said ruefully, "even when she

succeeds in making me feel like a veritable heel. It hasn't been easy for her. All her close friends have married—some already have children—while—well, it has seemed best to wait. Perhaps it is just stubbornness on my part as Sylvia insists; but in this I shall remain firm. I shall not marry until I can feel reasonably confident of the future."

"Of course not," Ruth said, "and she should understand your side of the situation or else——"

"Or else?" her brother repeated. "That's what I'm afraid of, I suppose," he said, "and yet I would be the last to blame her if she ditched me for another man. I know her parents never approved of me—especially her mother."

"If she could do that, then she doesn't love you, Bruce," Ruth told him, "and you would be well rid of her."

"You don't care for Sylvia especially, do you, Ruth?" he asked, eying his sister narrowly. "Oh, I know you are always pleasant when you meet but——"

"I probably like her just as much as she likes me," Ruth retorted quickly. "We live in different worlds. I'm a working woman, she is a lily of the field—and the twain can never see eye to eye. It just can't be done."

"I shall never understand my luck in winning her consent to become my wife, Ruth," the young man said, his voice dreamy. "She could have married any one of a dozen men— wealthy, established, handsome—some of them cultured and in her own set, and yet she chose me. There are times when it makes me almost humble——"

"Nonsense!" his sister cried impatiently. "You were a rising and popular young surgeon, and in your uniform you looked the answer to every girl's prayer. You could have had any girl you wanted and you know it. How long since you developed an inferiority complex, my conceited, self-satisfied brother?" she jibed.

He promptly boxed her ears, his face flushed. He was suddenly quite thoroughly and healthily ashamed of himself. They laughed together and the atmosphere cleared.

"How is Jill Ordway making out, Ruth?" he asked as he sorted the mail.

Ruth took the letter he handed her and slit the envelope before answering. "Fine, Bruce!" she told him. "She's still doing the work of three nurses, however." She slipped the envelope into her pocket and went on. "I shall be relieved when we are in a position to dispense with two or three more of our very incompetent helpers. If the three girls arrive when they promised we shall be in clover. And—— Oh, I nearly forgot to tell you; Mr. Allison was here yesterday, Bruce. He appeared quite enthusiastic when he heard our plans and is pleased with the results of his advertising campaign. He went through the buildings and made some constructive suggestions. The only thing is, they will require more money to carry them out than we can spare just at present. Still, we might consider them for the future. You haven't had so much to say about him lately. He's a friend of Jeff's, too, isn't he? They seemed to be very fond of each other. I rather liked what I saw of him. Is he wealthy, Bruce?"

"Oh, yes," her brother said, "and he's a friend of the Websters, too. In fact—well—I used to consider him a rather dangerous rival once upon a time. I think Sylvia's family favored Pete—but, well—you know how it is with young people. They make their own decisions. Pete's a swell fellow—none better. So he approves of the Kimberly Sanatorium? Sylvia won't like that."

With a gesture of helpless resignation, Ruth left the office and went about her duties. So Pete Allison was one of Sylvia's old beaux? Ruth shook her head and decided she didn't like him after all. She wondered why it was that men never seemed to look below the surface where a beautiful blonde was concerned. What was it Sylvia Webster had that—say, Jill Ordway, or Ann Burke, or even Ruth Kimberly didn't have more of—plus common sense, brains and integrity? And yet the finest, most eligible men passed them by with scarcely a glance to sit at the feet of a Sylvia Webster.

"Snap out of it, Ruth," she told herself as she mounted the stairs to the second floor. " 'Love goes where it's sent,' Madame Cartright used to tell us and she always added that, 'while men prefer blondes, they generally marry brunettes' or something of the sort. I suppose that was to give us dark gals hope." She laughed silently and called herself an idiot.

The fourteen patients in the sanatorium appeared to be making fair progress. Each was a distinct problem and had to be handled carefully and tactfully. Mrs. Botany still complained of Wilkes, the plump middle-aged nurse who was growing

43

increasingly weary of her fault-finding. Tim Woodworth was busy making purses now. He had tired of straight weaving and was experimenting quite successfully with other items. Jill Ordway encouraged him in every venture and had gradually learned much about the patient's personal life and habits. She hadn't told him of getting in touch with the Barry family in the little town of Blair's Corners, up-state, and that Mrs. Barry had promised to write Tim, inviting him to Blair's Corners for a long visit, and without letting him know anyone had told her to do so. And now this morning a letter had arrived addressed to Tim. She brought it to him and watched his face as he examined the envelope—the postmark and date.

"Why, I used to live in Blair's Corners, Nurse," he exclaimed excitedly. "I wonder who this is from. We left there years ago when I was just a youngster—twelve, I guess, and I never went back. Mom and the neighbor next door, Mrs. Barry, wrote back and forth for a while but I guess the friendship just naturally petered out. Let's see, there was a girl—Lolly—Laura her name was. We called her Lolly. She was a pretty kid—red hair and big brown eyes and freckles—gosh, what freckles! I used to tease her about them and she nearly took the skin off using everything she could find or hear of, trying to get rid of them. Poor kid! But she was pretty and good, too. I wonder whatever became of her. Probably married by this time with half a dozen kids. She was crazy about kids. Lolly Barry—I wonder if she'd remember me."

"Perhaps your letter is from her, Tim," Jill suggested. "Why don't you open it and see?"

He laughed shyly and slit the envelope, drawing out a folded sheet of paper covered with closely written lines. He read rapidly, his face gradually changing—brightening until he seemed to shed most of his twenty-seven years and was again a boy of twelve.

As he finished he held the letter aloft and cried, "Yippee! It's from Mrs. Barry—she wants me to come to visit them. She says she has been searching for me—knew of sis's death and tried to reach me then, but couldn't. When can I leave, Nurse? She wants me as soon as I can come." He paused and his face resumed its former somber expression. "You can't know what it has been to be all stark alone in the world, Miss Ordway. Not a soul who cared whether I lived or died."

44

"I haven't too many relatives myself, Tim," Jill told him. "I have an elder brother Jack, who brought me up. He has his wife and son and daughter; but I have no one, so I can appreciate something of your loneliness. But I have my work which I love and so I don't think about it—much."

"I know," the patient said. "But there are times when you do. You haven't answered me, Nurse. When can I leave?"

"Just as soon as you can walk down to the brook and back without having to go to bed for a day or two afterward," Jill told him. "You haven't been outside the building yet. This is a fine crisp fall day, Tim. Why not come out for a little stroll —just down to the gate and back? We can rest at both ends of the trip. How about it?"

The young man hesitated. The fear that had possessed him ever since he was rescued from the prison camp was not entirely dissipated. His hands clenched and he set his teeth as he rose from the chair in which he was sitting. He stood for a moment—a tall, emaciated figure, pathetic in its feebleness— then took a resolute step forward and then another.

"Okay," he said, his smile somewhat forced. "Let's go."

Jill laughed. "Wait, you must have an overcoat and hat and maybe gloves and overshoes. The ground is cold. I'll get them for you. You sit down again and wait for me."

She helped him dress and they walked slowly to the tiny elevator at the end of the corridor. Doctor Kimberly met them on the porch and stood aside to let them pass. Jill smiled at him.

"This is Tim's first trip into the wide-open spaces since he came to us, Doctor Kimberly. We're going down to the gate. Just a short journey this time."

"Don't go too far," the doctor warned. "Remember, for every step forward there must be a corresponding step back, or you will find yourselves stranded at the wrong end."

He watched the two—nurse and patient—as they made their slow, careful way down the brick walk to the imposing sanatorium gate where an iron bench stood against a giant elm. There they sat down for a moment before starting back. Doctor Kimberly nodded approval and went on inside. He mounted the stairs to the second floor and along the wide corridor to the room at the end where Bud Fowler lay in a condition barely conscious. He had been like this ever since he had arrived four days before, and Judson had prescribed electricity and radiation, neither of which had had any apparent effect. The patient rolled his head from side to side and his eyes were dark with pain. He seemed entirely unable to talk and made little or no effort to do so. His grandmother, who had accompanied him to the sanatorium, blamed his condition on the war, and yet he had suffered no injuries and but little real inconvenience, having been in the office of the paymaster the entire two years of his service.

X-rays showed nothing wrong with his body—no nerve pressure as far as could be detected, although both Bruce and Jeff were confident of pressure somewhere. Bruce was inclined to the theory of a brain tumor but Judson was definitely against it. At last, Bruce decided to consult Doctor Morley at the Center. Morley was the best surgeon in the locality and Bruce wanted his opinion. He had broached the matter to the grandmother only to have her raise vigorous objections. She had already obtained several medical and surgical opinions and nothing had been said about a brain tumor. Just why should the subject be brought up now? What the boy needed was rest and good nursing and she understood he could obtain both here in the Kimberly Sanatorium.

"True, Mrs. Fowler," the doctor assured her, "but I shall feel better if we have expert advice on the cause of your grandson's condition and I feel sure Morley is the man to give it."

"I understand that you are a surgeon, Doctor Kimberly," the old lady said. "Why can't you operate if you feel it necessary? I don't like Doctor Morley—too gruff—too opinionated."

"He's a good surgeon, though," Bruce contended, hesitating to explain his own inability to do the job. This morning he again reiterated his decision that an operation was imperative and that Morley was the man to do it.

"But why Morley? Why not you?" Mrs. Fowler demanded, and as Bruce shook his head, "Then I feel sure it isn't best," she said firmly.

"My dear lady," Bruce said grimly, "I should be only too happy to do it if I were able. But—well, I, too, am a war casualty." He held out his scarred right hand and with difficulty flexed the fingers. "I shall never be able to operate again, Mrs. Fowler; but my ability to diagnose is still as keen as ever. I

46

am willing to stake my reputation that your grandson is suffering from a brain tumor which is getting no better. Will you not trust me?''

The old lady's sharp blue eyes were bright with tears as she put out her hands and caught his. "My dear boy," she cried, "I didn't realize. I'm sure you know what is best. Call in your Doctor Morley; but I want you to promise me that you will be present during the operation. I shall feel Bud is safer that way.''

"Nothing could keep me away, Mrs. Fowler," Bruce told her, "and I feel sure he is going to be all right. Morley is a fine surgeon—if Bud were my own son or brother, Morley's the man I should pick to do the job.''

Was it possible or did the tall young man in the narrow bed appear to relax? Perhaps he only imagined it, but somehow Bruce Kimberly followed Mrs. Fowler from the room in a much better frame of mind.

Outside, the November sun was warm. The trees were quite bare now, with the exception of the firs whose foliage seemed to have darkened with the approach of winter. Red berries shone on the hedgerows bordering the drive, and a few hardy chrysanthemums flaunted their ragged heads as if daring any frost or icy winds to harm them. Doctor Kimberly watched Mrs. Fowler as she was helped into her limousine, and raised a hand in reply to her wave of farewell.

"How did she react to your insistence of immediate surgery this time, Bruce?" Ruth Kimberly asked as the two met in the lower hall.

"At first she was just as stubbornly opposed as ever but in the end she seemed perfectly willing her grandson should be examined by Morley and to accept his opinion, provided I be present during the operation. Of course I promised—wild horses couldn't keep me away. Morley is coming at two, Ruth. See that we're not disturbed.''

"Of course," Miss Kimberly agreed, a fleeting memory of Sylvia Webster's indignation the last time Bruce had been in conference and she had insisted he be called to the telephone immediately. She sincerely hoped history wouldn't repeat itself this time.

"BLAKE'S POND IS frozen over, Jill," Ann Burke said as they walked the short distance from the sanatorium to the nurses' home after lunch on a cold early December day. "How about getting in some skating this P.M.?"

"I don't even know if I can find my skates, Ann," Jill told her. "I don't remember packing them in my trunk, although, of course, they must be there. I'm not one to do a half-job of packing. It might be fun. I haven't skated since before the war. I'll look and see if I have my skates and we'll go early. It's a good mile out to the pond, isn't it?"

"Oh, not quite that far," Ann replied. "I walked over there the other day and it didn't seem far to me." They were silent for a moment and then Ann said tentatively, "Are you serious about Doctor Thomas, Jill? Of course, I know it is none of my business, but——"

Jill stood still and stared at the other nurse. "Serious, Ann? I? What on earth ails you? Why should I be serious about Jeff? I like him, of course; everyone likes him. But that's positively all. Why do you ask?"

Ann caught Jill's hand and they resumed their walk. "Oh, I sort of thought—you know, he seemed to like you a lot and I wondered."

"I suppose because we went dancing down in Westhaven one evening last week. That didn't mean a thing, Ann. Jeff was sort of bored and asked me to help break the monotony. After all, Jeff and you and I are the only young people here —I mean, *free* young people—and I suppose it could get sort of grim. If you had been off duty perhaps he would have asked you instead of me."

"Fat chance," Ann muttered. "The lug isn't even aware I'm alive. I think he's cute, Jill."

"He'd slay you if he heard you say that, Ann," Jill laughed. "But at that Jeff's a grand chap. I'm very fond of him. We're the best of friends, although there are times when he sort of gets in my hair."

"How do you mean?" Ann asked as they mounted the steps to the porch.

"Oh, he's always wanting to go somewhere. He calls it relaxing—needful recreation, but to me it's just a plain waste of time. You see, Ann, there is so much to be done here to make this place a success that I can't bear to fool around running hither and yon chasing after a dubious good time. But can you make Jeff understand that? You cannot. He takes me to task every little while over my sticking too closely to the job." She laughed dubiously as she shut the door and paused for a moment to pick up her mail from the hall table.

"I wish he'd invite me to go dancing or a movie sometime," Ann murmured more to herself than to Jill. "There are times when I can quite understand the attitude Cotten and Burtless take—about staying too long in a place——"

"That's because they don't take a personal interest in it, Ann," Jill said quickly. "To us who are determined to make the Kimberly Sanatorium a going concern there's nothing the least bit boring or monotonous about it here. I love it and nothing I can do to improve conditions will be too hard or too demanding."

Ann, who was halfway up the stairs, paused to ask slyly, "And just what do you expect to get out of all this devotion, my love? Have you, by any chance, money invested in the project, or is there some ulterior motive? Oh, I'm sorry, darling. I was only ribbing you. And I like the Kimberlys myself. They're a grand pair. I don't think I shall be able to say as much if and when Doc takes on the Webster gal for a wife. I just can't stand her."

"Do you know Sylvia, Ann?" Jill asked in some surprise. "From the way you spoke the other day I thought——"

"Oh, but since then I've heard an earful. She's a snob of the first water, and if Doc marries her, believe me there will be a For Sale sign on this dump pronto. Someone told me she's been putting a bug in the collective ears of the Hospital Board —wants them to take the place over—declare it superfluous —infringing on their territory, so to speak. You know, of course, or don't you? Old man Tillotson's not only president of the board but the biggest stockholder as well."

"So what? And who may this Tillotson be, Ann? Just what can he do?"

49

"Why, he's the Webster gal's uncle and godfather—bad cess to 'im! He's got all the money in the world outside the national debt—and I'm willing to bet that half of that belongs to him. It seems he's eccentric—in other words, more than a little crazy. His infatuation for that one proves it and he should have been confined years ago."

"I think you're making all this up," Jill said. "The Kimberlys own this sanatorium. I know that. Kim's an accredited physician and his sister's a registered nurse, The place is endorsed by both county and state and I doubt if anyone can force its discontinuance. Where do you hear such tales, Ann? I don't think there can be a grain of truth in it."

"Maybe not, Jill," Ann retorted. "I'm only repeating what I've heard. The Websters, *et al*, are powerful in these parts and when they are reinforced by Tillotson and more of that ilk, there's no knowing what they may be capable of doing. I, for one, am keeping my fingers crossed. Now forget the job, darling. Let's relax and have ourselves a time." They parted and Jill, frowning slightly, called herself an idiot for giving the matter a single serious thought. But she determined to have a talk with Ruth Kimberly at the first opportunity.

The day was crisp and cold with not too much snow. The two girls trudged briskly along the frozen highway, the ice crackling with every step. They expected to find the pond deserted this early in the afternoon, but that was not the case. From some distance away they could see the huge bonfire at one end of the pond, which was in fact a small lake, and around it stood groups of people, their laughter and shouts ringing in the frosty air. A sprinkling of skaters were circling the ice singly and in pairs and the two girls quickened their pace. People smiled at them but no one spoke and they sat down on a nearby bench to change their shoes. As if at a signal, a young man detached himself from the fire worshipers and offered his services. He was a tall, rugged young man with a ruddy face and keen blue eyes.

"You're strangers around here, aren't you?" he asked as he pulled the zipper on Ann's boots. "Okay—next?" He smiled into Jill's gray eyes and reached for her white boots. "Laced. Good! I like them better than the others—adjust better."

"Oh, you do," Ann pouted. "Well, as it happens, I prefer mine. We're nurses at the Kimberly Sanatorium," she explained, kicking at the ice with the toe of one skate. "You live around here?"

"Sure," he replied. "I'm Alan Blake—this pond is on my property!"

"Horrors! Then we're trespassing," Ann cried in mock terror. "How awful! And we never asked your leave—Mr. Blake. What are you going to do with us?"

"Oh, that's all right," the young man said, tying a knot in Jill's shoelace. "Everyone uses this pond in winter and comes here to fish in summer. I'm not one to object to people using my property if they know how to behave themselves." He laughed shyly, showing large, very white teeth. "There you are, young lady. Have a good time. We have hot coffee over here any time you feel like it. What did you say your names are?" he asked, his eyes on Jill, whose hand Ann held preparatory to starting out on a long swing around the pond. Ann answered.

"Did we say?" she teased. "I don't remember."

But Jill took pity on him and said pleasantly, "I am Jill Ordway and this is Ann Burke, and thank you for helping us. We'll be seeing you again—I hope."

"Why did you tell him?" Ann demanded as they skated off, aware of the interested gaze of some score or more curious people. "It might have been fun keeping him in the dark— being mysterious. I've always wanted to be mysterious, but someone is usually spoiling it," she sighed gustily. "He was rather nice, wasn't he? I wonder if he's married or—involved in any way."

Jill laughed. "Why don't you ask him?"

"I might at that. He's a sort of neighbor and might prove useful—at times."

And on this same afternoon, Sylvia Webster's smart blue roadster stopped before the Kimberly Sanatorium. She sat for a moment, her eyes on the somewhat bleak snow-covered landscape, before she got out, reached for the leash of a huge mastiff and together they walked to the porch and waited while Sylvia rang the bell. It was some time until the maid appeared and the visitor grew restive. The door opened at last and without a word Sylvia swept haughtily into the foyer, pulling the reluctant dog after her.

"Animals are not permitted inside the sanatorium, Miss," Molly Foster told her, holding the door wide so that the dog could leave. "I'm sorry; and there's a sign near the gate——"

Sylvia ignored her protest and continued down the hall to Doctor Kimberly's office. It was empty and she sat down, the dog beside her, and waited impatiently. Molly went in search of Miss Kimberly. She told her story and Ruth hastened to the chief's office. She greeted Sylvia cordially and then reiterated that animals were not allowed inside the grounds, as some of the patients were allergic to them.

Sylvia said coolly, "This is a present for Bruce, Ruth. King is a very special dog and I went to great trouble and expense getting him. I know Bruce loves dogs and I thought he would enjoy having King. I have his papers—he has a fine pedigree——"

"That was thoughtful of you, Sylvia," Ruth interrupted, "but you know, in a place like this, one can't have dogs roaming about, frightening nervous patients and——"

"But King isn't just a common dog, Ruth," Sylvia pointed out. "He's very special—Bruce will adore him, I know. Let us wait until he comes and let him decide. I'm sure King is going to be a joy to him." She paused a moment, then went on, "Do you know anything at all about dogs, Ruth? Would you recognize a thoroughbred if you should see one?"

Ruth Kimberly smiled. "I love all dogs, Sylvia," she said. "From the commonest mongrel to the most aristocratic of the species. It's a trait of the family, and it is one of the sacrifices we have had to make for our profession, especially since acquiring our sanatorium. We don't mind too much——"

"The sanatorium!" Sylvia sneered, her lip curling in distaste.

"Don't you like it?" Ruth asked, although she knew the place was an anathema to Sylvia. "Bruce and I have grown quite fond of it and we feel we are making headway. Already we have been able to discharge three patients—give them a clean bill of health—steady nerves and a happy outlook for the future. It has all been so worth while, especially so when I look at Bruce and note the marked improvement in his condition.'"

"How can you say that, Ruth Kimberly?" the visitor demanded angrily, and the huge mastiff got to his feet and moved away. Ruth reached out and patted his head and he moved closer to her. Sylvia tightened her grip on his leash and he sat down on his haunches, then gradually lay down, his massive head between his paws. "Bruce isn't the same man he was before he went to war and you know it."

"Of course I do, Sylvia. None of us is the same. War does things to a person and Bruce was particularly hard hit—the loss of his career in surgery, his nerve shock and——"

"That's what I mean," Sylvia interrupted. "This place is the very worst thing in the world for him. He should have freedom from worry—the need to watch queer people with crazy notions. He needs gayety—sunshine—entertainment—to be associated with normal, healthy people."

Ruth shook her head. Her brown eyes were serious, her mouth unsmiling. "What Bruce needs now is work—plenty of it. Work is God's gift to a restless, unhappy world," she said quietly. "I know, because I have experienced its blessings."

For a moment the girl opposite said nothing. The hands on the leash moved nervously and King raised his head inquiringly, then dropped it again.

"When do you expect Bruce back?" she asked at last, pulling back her cuff to look at her watch. "And by the way, just where is he? He usually tells me if he intends going out of town."

"Bruce is with a patient in the hospital right now," Ruth said, her eyes on her wrist watch. "He should be back almost any minute."

"At City Hospital? Can't he handle his patients here?" It was asked almost contemptuously and Ruth explained that the boy's grandmother wanted Bruce to be present during the operation. Sylvia laughed scornfully. "And just why should he be at the beck and call of every old woman who wants him to act as nursemaid to her child, Ruth? It's undignified—it's positively ridiculous and I won't have it."

"I don't imagine you will have anything to do with that particular phase of my brother's work, Sylvia," Ruth said sharply. "The boy has, or had, a brain tumor. It required a very delicate operation and one in which Bruce has been especially successful. The grandmother knew this and wanted him to operate; but of course he couldn't, so he suggested Doctor Morley at the Center for the job and promised to be present during the ordeal."

"Bruce might better have gone into private practice or be-

53

come a diagnostician at the Center as I have repeatedly urged him to do. They were keen to have him there. He could have built up a fine following and with our connections it wouldn't have taken too long. It would certainly have been less sordid —more dignified."

Ruth shook her head. "Sordid? Well, perhaps some of our cases could be classed as rather sordid, only we don't see them as such. We find each one vastly interesting and experience a thrill of accomplishment when the patient shows improvement —when taut nerves relax—the mind slowly reacts to certain special therapeutics—the general health picks up and we once again return a man or woman to his or her family a normal, active human being. I assure you there is nothing quite like it. We feel amply repaid—aside from whatever fee involved."

Sylvia was unimpressed, but before she could say anything, a car came up the drive and stopped before the porch. Bruce got out and mounted the broad steps two at a time. King arose and stood with his feet braced as if defying the newcomer to advance. Doctor Kimberly opened the door and for a moment stood rooted to the spot.

Before he greeted his sister or fiancée he asked sharply, "Who let that dog in here? Oh, hello, darling. Is he yours? Well, you can't bring him here, you know. No dogs or animals of any species are allowed inside these sacred walls—inside the fence for that matter. Better get him out before word gets around, Sylvia." He snapped the fingers of his left hand at King, who sniffed inquisitively, then wagged his tail. "How long have you been a dog lover?" he asked, grinning at the girl.

"He's yours, Bruce," Sylvia said, her lip trembling, her wide blue eyes pleading. "I got him for your birthday. Don't you like him? I went to such a lot of trouble—and expense—to get him. He's a thoroughbred, darling. I have his papers. His name is King and off here in the country like you are you need protection—King to guard you."

Bruce shouted with laughter and the dog strained at his leash. Ruth marveled at the change in the girl's voice. It was charming, beautiful, almost alluring in its girlish appeal. She sighed.

"Call this country?" Bruce chided. "And what do I need of a bodyguard? Don't be crazy, my dear. You need him far more

54

than I do, so you keep him—he's a splendid fellow. Only I warn you, don't ever bring him here again. We don't allow animals of any kind in this place—not even a cat. Now, out you go—both of you. I hate being inhospitable, darling, but I'm a busy man—thank God—and this is a sanatorium, remember."

"I'm not likely to forget," the girl said stiffly. "Your sister has been pounding that fact into my apparently dumb brain for the past hour. Oh, I'll go. Come on, King, we're not welcome here." She left the room without a backward glance, shoulders stiff, head high. Bruce muttered something and followed. Ruth went up the stairs, leaving them alone.

"Don't be mad at me, darling," Doctor Kimberly pleaded, his arm about the unyielding shoulders. King rubbed against his legs and Bruce's hand patted the massive head. "It was sweet of you to think of me and I do appreciate it; but rules are rules, sweet, and our patients must always come first."

"I see," the girl answered. "Before even me. I have to take second place—or third or fourth for all I know. I don't like it, Bruce. You seem to be growing farther and farther away from me. How will it end?"

"Don't be silly," the man protested, catching her in his arms and holding her close while King looked on, a bored expression on his broad face. At last he yawned widely and lay down. Sylvia sighed wistfully.

"Couldn't you keep King at your own house, Bruce? He's a well-bred, beautifully trained dog. He needn't bother your patients and——"

Bruce drew back from her arms. He frowned and his lips were firm as he shook his head. "No," he said uncompromisingly. "No dogs—no animals are allowed on the premises. Didn't you read the sign on the gatepost? It says plainly that animals of all kinds are prohibited and that means King, too. No, darling, you keep him with you. I'll see him when I come to see you. Now I've got to ask you to excuse me. Good-bye, sweet. Take care of yourself—and you should with King on guard. But by the way, isn't he supposed to be a watch dog? How come he let me manhandle you?" He laughed as he asked the question, and King wagged his tail.

"He knows we both belong to you, darling," Sylvia explained. "I told him all about you and he thoroughly approves, don't you, King?" King yawned and Bruce grinned at him. He opened the door and stood until the two had left the porch and then he turned and raced up the stairs. Upon looking back, Sylvia was annoyed not to find him watching her and she gave a vicious tug on King's leash and the huge animal promptly sat down and refused to budge, so that she had literally to haul him to the car. Her expression was anything but happy as she drove back to town. She had banked on Bruce's love of animals to gradually bind him more closely to her. She gazed at the intelligent King and shook her head.

"We shall have to try something else, old man," she muttered as she swung into the city traffic.

## 8

Bud Fowler was conscious when Bruce Kimberly made an early morning visit to City Hospital on the day following the operation. The sunken eyes were open and shone wanly in his thin face. He smiled at his caller and held out a wasted hand.

"Good—work—Doctor," he said haltingly. "I—knew——"

"Doctor Morley's a fine surgeon, Bud," Bruce told him.

"But—it—was—you—did—it—actually," the patient insisted. "I—felt—you—there——"

Bruce smiled, his eyes warm. "We were all pulling for you, son. Better take it easy—rest—relax—very little talking for a while. I'll be in again."

He hurried back to the sanatorium, his heart singing. It was almost as if he had actually done the job himself. Bud had felt that way too and he was going to be all right. Oh, it was good to be busy again! Good to feel he was accomplishing something. His blood tingling from the cold, he entered the dimly lighted lower hall—saw no one and mounted the stairs at his usual pace of two steps at once and collided with Jill Ordway as he turned a corner in the upper corridor. He caught her two shoulders to steady her as she tottered uncertainly for a moment after the impact.

"What's the rush, Doctor?" she asked as he released her. "And tell me about the operation. Was it successful? It *was* a tumor, of course," she said breathlessly, and bit her lip to steady her nerves.

"You're a great pepper-upper to the old ego, Jill," he said, grinning down at her. "But as it happened there was a tumor —a fairly good-sized one at that, and it was removed beautifully—I couldn't have done it better myself. But I'm telling you, it took every bit of will power I possessed to watch calmly while Morley did the job. I wanted to shove him aside and take over. But he did a swell job and Bud is back in his room, his grandmother already in close attendance. She kissed me when the job was over and gave me her blessing. You know, the boy is all she has—the last of the line, she told me." He sighed and murmured almost wistfully, "It was almost like old times, scrubbing there with Morley and comparing notes while listening to the internes and nurses arguing back and forth in the adjoining washrooms. I always liked City Hospital, although most of my work was done at the Center. Been over there yet, Jill?"

Jill nodded. "Yes," she replied. "Jeff took me there before I came out here, else"—she smiled—"I doubt if I should have seen it at all. It's a huge place, isn't it? I liked the Center, too, especially the operating rooms—they're so modern—up-to-date. I met a lot of the doctors and nurses, too. They were all very friendly—quite willing to show me everything. Believe me, when Jeff pilots one about, he does a thorough job of it."

Doctor Kimberly murmured something unintelligible, then asked, "How long have you known Jeff Thomas, Jill? I never heard you speak of him—or for that matter, I have never heard him mention you. Are you old friends?"

"At least we are friends—I hope," Jill smiled. "Jeff's a peach, Kim—Doctor. He has been mighty sweet to me since I have been here. No, I haven't known him very long as one measures time—it isn't how long but how well one knows a person that counts."

"I see," Bruce said, and went on along the corridor to room 29 where sixteen-year-old Nancy Meredith, suffering from major chorea and wearing herself out with her continued restlessness, was waiting for him. Doctor Kimberly was using a new treatment and watching her closely. Ann Burke, nurse in attendance, was confident of improvement and reported the slight, almost imperceptible lessening of the oscillations. The girl greeted him shyly and tried desperately to remain quiet. The effort was tremendous and Bruce smiled his sympathy. They were good friends, these two—the girl shyly adoring the tall, good-looking doctor and the young man admiring the dauntless courage of the frail girl. Her nurses reported her unfailing cheerfulness and called her a model patient. She had been unable to attend school since adolescence and even the special tutoring her parents provided had been stopped after her entrance into Kimberly. Bruce had his own ideas as to the therapy best adapted to her particular case.

Now as he examined her chart he felt a return of the exhilaration experienced when making that early morning call on Bud Fowler, which was partly and unaccountably dashed after talking with Jill Ordway. He was on the right track—they had something really worth while in this treatment being used. Things were shaping up nicely here.

Everyone in the sanatorium was interested in the outcome of Bud Fowler's operation and there was general rejoicing at the favorable report. Ruth Kimberly felt their stock bounded upward when the news leaked out. But over the west wing there hung a shadow. Minna Blazer was not an old patient—she was young and her stay at Kimberly had been brief—two weeks to be exact. But again the staff was interested in her particular case because of her extreme youth and the apparent hopelessness of her condition. Just this morning it had been found necessary to transfer Minna to the State Hospital for the Insane and Bruce Kimberly was unhappy at his inability to help her.

"Some day we shall know just how to cope with such cases," he said despondently when the patient had gone. "Some day there will be no incurable mental cases. I feel very strongly about this, Ruth. The little Blazer girl should not have been allowed to reach her present condition. Thank God it won't be long for her. If I could have had her earlier——"

"You would, in all probability, not have been especially interested in her then, Bruce," his sister reminded him. "In those days you had but one thought—surgery. But in a way I can appreciate her family's attitude. The idea of putting her away was abhorrent to them. They hoped she would outgrow her nervousness—most girls do—and so they let her drift along, hoping against hope that a miracle would occur. And now it is

58

too late. But, as you say, I don't imagine it will be very long. There have been increasing evidences that her heart is weakening. Poor child! There are so many worse things than death —which so often proves itself a friend in disguise—leading to freedom. I don't think you need have any regrets, Bruce. You tried—against the advice of several older and more experienced men—and failed. But at least you tried—that's something in your favor."

"I know, but it shows me how really helpless we are—how little we actually know about the mind—what small headway the profession has made in the care and treatment of mental diseases. It's a wide and interesting field, Ruth, and one I intend spending my life exploring. I wish—— Oh, let it ride. King's a splendid animal, isn't he?" he asked tentatively.

"He is, dear, and I wish we—you could keep him."

"Well, I can't. That's out. Sylvia should have known it, too. But the Winslows' dogs made such a hit with me that I suppose she thought a dog was just the thing I would enjoy. She is always doing things like that—trying to please me."

Ruth Kimberly said nothing aloud, but she had her own thoughts and they were certainly not altogether complimentary to Miss Webster. However, she had long ago made up her mind to do nothing to open her brother's eyes to the selfishness of the beauteous Sylvia. She knew the girl didn't like her —knew that she was unsympathetic with the engagement, although she was always sweetly cordial when Bruce was around and the reverse when he was not. But being older than Sylvia, though four years her brother's junior, Ruth refused to take offense at anything the girl said or did. She hoped with all her heart that something would happen to break the unfortunate engagement. Since the advent of Jill Ordway she had been somewhat easier in her mind. She had a faint suspicion, although she told herself there was not the least proof to warrant it, that Jill Ordway was in love with Bruce and she thought how wonderful it would be if they could marry. Jill was a girl after her own heart. She had liked her voice, she had liked Bruce's description of their relationship, she had not been disappointed when they at last met. Now that they were working together her admiration and liking had strengthened. She had reached the conclusion that Jill Ordway was the girl for her adored brother.

59

But what about Jeff Thomas—the irrepressible and likable young research enthusiast who seemed enamored of Jill? Did Jill care for him? They were very friendly. She had a feeling that Ann Burke favored Jeff and wished she dared encourage them, but of course she could not. She was making unheard of concessions in allowing any friendly relations at all between male and female members of the staff. She laughed to herself. Inasmuch as Judson was married and very much in love with his pretty wife, and Bruce was already engaged, that left Doctor Thomas the sole eligible male among some dozen females. Of course several of the nurses were already married and there were two bachelor consultants who made frequent calls at the sanatorium and were not only willing but eager to date the nurses, and then three or four Westhaven men with matrimonial intentions who made weekly calls at the nurses' home and according to Mrs. Davis, the housemother, kept them out far too late at night. Still, they were rather far out and there was not much in the way of fun and recreation—especially at this time of the year. In summer there would be tennis, croquet, baseball and even golf if the girls wanted to trudge the mile to the municipal links. Also, a little later, when there should be more snow, skiing on the hills to the west. But just now there seemed little in the way of amusement to offer the staff. She sighed, then smiled. With success would come greater advantages—more attractive possibilities. Pete Allison had predicted a boom year and maybe he was a true prophet. Once again she revised her opinion of Pete. He was very likeable— he had invited her to have dinner with him some evening and she had made excuses. He had appeared disappointed. She sighed again. This being superintendent of a sanatorium—being largely responsible for its success—was no sinecure.

It was after dinner that evening when Jill Ordway stopped Ruth in the doorway of her small office on the ground floor and asked if she could spare a few minutes.

They sat down across the desk from each other and Jill said, "I'm sure you don't listen to gossip, Miss Kimberly, any more than I do—usually; but recently I have heard something that has worried me—knowing how very hard both you and your brother have been working to make this place a success. Do you mind if I talk to you about it? I realize it is none of my business—not really; but I, too, am interested in the sanatorium, for I know what it means to K—Doctor Kimberly."

Ruth smiled into the serious gray eyes of the girl opposite and said cordially, "Of course, Jill—I think of you as Jill because Bruce has talked so much about you. And when we are alone, won't you call me Ruth? I'm not really old and severe, although I know I must often appear to be."

"Thank you, Ruth," Jill said impulsively. "Could the City Hospital—the Center or even the doctors here close this place —term it superfluous—infringing on their practice, and so on? I have heard there is such a move impending to discredit Kimberly and I wondered if it was just talk or if there was actually some such idea abroad. I felt the best way to quash such rumors was to come to headquarters for the truth."

Ruth Kimberly shook her head. "This is all news to me, Jill. Bruce and I own this place, every stick and stone, every blade of grass and every brick—aside from an outsized mortgage which doesn't worry us unduly. We have the approval of both County and State Boards, so how could any group or individual discredit us?"

"I don't know. Who is this Tillotson and just how much harm is he capable of doing—if any?"

"Sam Tillotson? Oh, he's a wealthy eccentric—related to the Websters, I believe. Oh! I think I get a faint glimmer through the dark of this mystery. So that's it. Well, I'm sure even Sam Tillotson would think twice before attempting any shenanigans where we are concerned. Don't give the matter another thought, my dear. Considering the probable source I'm not in the least worried. How are things shaping up with you, Jill? Are we working you too hard? The new nurses appear to be doing very well, don't they? I hope they will decide to stay on with us."

"Oh, they like it here," Jill said. "Jeff—Doctor Thomas has been showing them the advantages of living in the country. He is taking two of them skating over on Blake's Pond tomorrow afternoon—on their time off duty. The skating is excellent over there and the people are so friendly. Ann and I were over there yesterday afternoon—a fire, hot coffee and plenty of partners. Don't people have to work in this part of the world?"

"I wouldn't know," Ruth said. "Why?"

"Oh, there must have been a dozen or more young men in

their early twenties having a good time when we were there. Alan Blake owns the place and enjoys having crowds around him. A very pleasant person. We thoroughly enjoyed ourselves."

"They tell me the skiing is good around here a bit later," Ruth said. "Do you ski, Jill?"

"I used to at college, but I haven't done any of it lately. I was surprised that I hadn't forgotten how to skate—it has been so long since I had a pair on. But I got along all right. I guess that's one of the things once learned is never quite forgotten."

"To get back to the sanatorium again, Jill," Ruth Kimberly smiled. "It isn't ever very far from my thoughts, you see. We are having a very special guest arriving tomorrow morning. He is Doctor Seth Bradley—a distinguished Presbyterian minister in search of rest and quiet. It seems he has been serving a large church in the Middle West for the past quarter century and is on the verge of collapse. His doctor ordered hospitalization or a nursing home but he heard of our sanatorium and decided to come here. It appears he wanted to retire but his congregation won't hear of it. Instead they have given him a six months' leave of absence. He isn't an old man exactly—somewhere in his fifties, I imagine. Pete—Mr. Allison spoke of him as a handsome, middle-aged gentleman, cultured and delightful to know. It seems he isn't exactly sick—except perhaps mentally—he's just tired—worn out and who wouldn't be after twenty-five years listening to the woes of several hundred people? I want you to look after him, Jill. He is to have a suite in the south wing where there is plenty of sun."

"Thank you, Ruth. I think I shall enjoy taking care of him. You mean he needs a full-time nurse? But if he isn't ill——"

"I know, but his wife—and congregation—insist that he have a special nurse and are paying generously for that service, so we are willing to give him our extra special nurse." She smiled affectionately and Jill glowed with pleasure.

As she left the office she wondered again at the gossip Ann had imparted and shook her head. Of course it was all nonsense. It would certainly be tragic if anything happened to the sanatorium right now when everything was shaping up so wonderfully. And of course nothing would. She wondered if Ruth really had an idea of the instigator of the plot. From the way she spoke, one would almost think so, and discounted his or her ability to accomplish much.

"I have an idea Ruth isn't very happy over her brother's engagement," Jill said to herself as she walked over to the nurses' home a few minutes later. She drew her cape more closely about her body and quickened her steps. She was suddenly cold and very tired and as she mounted the steps of the dimly lighted house in which she had lived for the past two months she wondered if she had done a wise thing in coming here. The future, as she saw it, held nothing but hard work and heartache for her; but perhaps the one would compensate for the other. She drew a deep breath of the sharp winter air and stood for a moment with tilted head, somber eyes on the starry sky. "Dear God," she prayed silently, "help me to carry on— give me strength and courage to meet each day with a high heart and unswerving devotion, unworried and unafraid of whatever the future may have in store."

In the west a meteor swept along the broad expanse of blue-blackness in an arc of light. Jill went inside and up to her room. She must think that whatever happened was for the best. At least she had Kim's friendship—she had helped him regain his health and courage and no matter what the future brought she had the weeks and months of close companionship when he had clung to her. Nothing could take that memory from her.

9

DOCTOR BRADLEY WAS a rather small man with a round pleasant face in which only the dark eyes held a trace of sadness. His thick curly hair was nearly white, and he had a nervous habit of thrusting his fingers through it from time to time. He arrived alone and was welcomed by both Bruce Kimberly and his sister in a manner intended to give him a feeling of warmth and understanding. He was pleased with his rooms and with his nurse and sank gratefully into the comfortable chair in the sunny window with a sigh of relief.

"I can rest here," he said after a moment when, with closed eyes, his head against the back of his chair, he smiled in the general direction of his nurse. "I am so tired—so very tired. Not ill, you understand, just tired. I shall try not to become a nuisance. If you find me too demanding or not co-operative enough—just remind me of my shortcomings and I shall reform instantly—I hope." His dark eyes opened suddenly and he gazed at her in something like wonder. "You don't mind attending me, do you?" he asked almost shyly.

"On the contrary, I am happy for anything I can do to make you comfortable, Doctor Bradley. I feel honored that I was chosen for the job. I wish you would feel free to use me in any capacity—nurse, companion, secretary, general cheerer-upper, if you like. I'm rather a cheerful person, though I hope not offensively so. From your case history I find your diet isn't too restricted. We have excellent food here and I shall try to make your meals attractive and interesting."

"But I shall not require special meals, Nurse," he remonstrated. "I can eat just about what the rest of you do. I don't want you to spend your time cooking for me. In fact, I won't have it. I believe I need rest more than food, anyway. Rest and understanding companionship. I feel confident Kimberly can provide both and I am content."

Bruce Kimberly had entered the sunny sitting room and stood for a moment listening to the patient's ultimatum. He smiled sympathetically.

"In other words, Nurse," he said, "Doctor Bradley wants and expects to have his own way while with us. Right, Doctor?"

"Right," the newcomer said. "I'm a little ashamed of being here at all. Ashamed of being compelled to give up when there is so much to be done, but——"

"Forget it," Bruce said firmly. "Look upon this brief respite as a quite necessary refueling—recharging a run-down battery —refreshing jaded nerves, if you please. It is a delightful country about here—interesting walks when weather permits; skating, if you enjoy skating, on a pond not too far away; drives into the hills and pleasant entertainment in the city two miles or more back along the main highway. Why, we even have access to a horse and sleigh, with real bells—delightful bells. I'm sure you will find your stay with us pleasant and profitable. At least we shall endeavor to make it so."

"Say no more, Doctor. My nurse and I understand each

64

other and I intend making the most of my enforced vacation. Don't give me a thought. I am not at all ill, you understand—just weary. It will pass—it must pass. I am not ready for the scrap pile yet, not by a long shot."

"At fifty-five!" Bruce smiled. "Well, scarcely. Even if I can do nothing for you, there are those here who are not so fortunate." His gaze swerved to Jill who was standing near the small desk at the opposite side of the room. "One thing we *have* done for you, Doctor Bradley, is to give you our favorite nurse—Miss Ordway. She it was who—literally—brought me back from the very gates of death—the brink of Hell, I nearly said, for that is what it amounts to; only she and I know what superhuman effort it took to set me on the way to health and happiness again."

"Peter Allison told me something about your injury, Doctor, and the subsequent blasting of your career in surgery," the clergyman said. "But you are to be congratulated. Not every casualty has been able to adjust himself to civilian life so happily. But then, not many have had such a charming aide—such delightful incentive."

Jill felt her heart pound and the blood rush to her temples. She reached for a magazine and riffled its pages. What must Kim think? She must disabuse her patient of any misconception of the relationship between Bruce and herself. She wished Kim would go. Suddenly she found his presence in the room embarrassing. And as if sensing her perturbation, Doctor Kimberly left. It was then Jill heard a faint chuckle from Doctor Bradley who was eying her amusedly.

"Don't mind me, my dear," he said smilingly. "My own young people are used to my somewhat pointed remarks and find them merely amusing. Your young doctor is a fine man —worthy of anything you have done or may do for him."

"But—but, Doctor Bradley," Jill cried, close to tears. "Kim —Doctor Kimberly is not *my* doctor. He is and has been for a long time engaged to Sylvia Webster—a beautiful and wealthy girl in Westhaven. Oh—how—how could you?"

"Wh-at? I don't understand," the man stammered. "I understood—I'm sure I understood—— Believe me, my dear, I am horrified at my stupidity. I have hurt you and I am deeply grieved. Will you forgive me? I assure you it will never happen again."

Jill gulped and swallowed with difficulty. "It's all right, Doctor," she replied, smiling thinly. "It wasn't your fault you were misinformed. I only hope—— Never mind. It's over and let's forget it, shall we? And now I am going to lower the shades and turn back your bed and you are going to have a nice, long nap before lunch." She went into the next room and proceeded to make it ready for her patient. She unpacked his bags, disposing the contents in closet and drawers, turned back the covers of the comfortable bed, laying out a gay, warm robe and slippers before returning to the sitting room.

"Everything is ready, Doctor," she told him cheerfully, "and if you need me you have only to call. I shall be right here. We usually have lunch at one—but you are privileged and may have yours at any time you wish."

The man walked toward the other room, then turned as he reached the door to say quietly, "I feel deeply grateful that you were assigned to me, my dear. I hope our relationship will improve as we go on together. I eat a very light lunch in the middle of the day—soup, a few crackers—perhaps a sweet bun or roll, and tea—my people were English," he smiled, and went in, leaving the door ajar.

"You're a sweetheart," Jill said to herself as she sat down, her patient's case history on the desk before her. "Blundering in spite of your years of training and experience, but kind and sympathetic. Perhaps association with you is just what I need —perhaps we are going to help each other." She thought of her frantic appeal to God on the night before and wondered if this might not be the answer—the help she so sorely needed.

At Christmas, Mrs. Bradley paid a visit to her husband and by special arrangement stayed at the sanatorium. A Christmas tree with small gifts for all stood in the wide entrance hall. Smaller trees had been prepared and set up in certain of the rooms where patients were unable to leave their beds and the whole place wore an air of festivity in keeping with the season. The main dining room was attractively decorated with holly and ground pine. A huge turkey graced one end of the laden table and Doctor Bradley sat at the head. Ruth Kimberly and the clergyman's wife on either side. Bruce Kimberly was absent. Sylvia had demanded his presence at the Tillotson festivities and much against his better judgment he made his excuses to the others and joined his fiancée at the mansion of her god-father. Unknown to each other, both Ruth Kimberly and Jill Ordway wished for some mysterious power that would transport them to that dinner—that would make them invisible to the others but would let them listen to what went on in that room.

Almost as if he had much the same desire, Doctor Bradley said to Ruth, "I have a commission from two of my parishioners to visit a Mr. Samuel Tillotson while I am here. It seems they are old-time friends and have been out of touch for years. I think while my wife is here we will take care of the matter so that she can make a report when she returns home."

But Jill, who had heard nothing of this conversation, was wondering if the question of scrapping Kimberly, or disposing of it in some way, had been broached at the Tillotson dinner. She knew Sylvia was opposed to Bruce's being associated with it and she knew also that the girl would probably stop at nothing to gain her objective. She was rich and beautiful and the potency of that combination was incalculable. And on the other hand, a man in love was apt to be vulnerable and she knew Bruce was very much in love with Sylvia Webster. She sighed and shook her head.

"What was that for?" Ann Burke wanted to know as she helped herself to a piece of white meat and plenty of stuffing. "You've been in a daze ever since we came down to dinner. Wake up! It's Christmas, or didn't you know? I only hope the ambulatory patients aren't going to suffer because of these unrestricted festivities. Did you see Mrs. Botany, Jill? Gosh, but she was a sketch! I bet she paid plenty for that dress—creation—she had on—when she bought it at least forty years ago. She insisted I go in and feel the material when I stood outside her room waiting for Jo Elliott. She's a queer old duck, isn't she? Rich as mud, they tell me. Well, one would never guess it to look at her. Where's Jeff dining, Jill? Do you know?"

"He told me he had received an invitation to dine with the paying guests, but said he preferred a tray in the lab. I saw the tray and—brother! he certainly stands in with the help. How are you and he getting along, Ann?" Jill asked, gazing blandly at her friend.

Ann blushed rosily. "How do you mean—getting along? I'm working on him, Jill, but he's cagey—shies off from my subtle approaches."

Jill laughed. "You just imagine it, Ann. He was asking about you only yesterday—last night when he walked me over to the house. Now what was it he wanted to know? M'm'm—I've forgotten."

Ann Burke swung around in her chair and caught Jill by the shoulders. "I could wring your neck with pleasure, Jill Ordway," she said fiercely. "He never did—never mentioned my name and you know it. Or—did he? Honest?"

Jill nodded, her eyes roguish.

"Then tell me—you've got to remember. Don't be mean, Jill. Please tell me. I need to know——"

"He wanted to know about your home—your family—your friends. It seems he sort of noticed you before you came here. He must have been attracted because he knew you had a room at the Y and were in private work. I told him what I knew and—well, that's all. Eat your dinner, Ann. Everyone's looking at you."

"You're not spoofing, Jill? Cross your heart—hope to see the back of your neck?"

Jill laughed again and held up her right hand. "I believe the lug admires you, Ann," she said softly. "But don't rush him—let him take his own time. As you say, Jeff's cagey and can't be maneuvered as some men can. More power to you, darling. He's a grand boy."

"Boy? He's somewhere in his thirties—must be to have reached the spot he's in now. Probably thirty-four or five—ten years my senior. H'm—just about right. He and the Chief were in Medical together, weren't they? Seems to me I heard something of the sort."

"I think so," Jill answered, suddenly withdrawn. Just what might be going on over at the Tillotson mansion? She would certainly like to know—or would she? She shivered and reached for her water glass.

And over in the elaborate dining room of the mansion in which dwelt Samuel H. Tillotson and a corps of servants, the meal was progressing slowly. The host, a widower of long standing, picked at his food and favored his guests with only occasional glances, none of which was especially pleasant. Mr. Tillotson suffered from stomach ulcers and looked at the world through somber glasses. His affection, if any, for his godchild was never very apparent to any but the girl herself, and was especially invisible this afternoon.

Sylvia, however, was at her most scintillating best. Her frock was ravishing, her hairdo attractive and her blue eyes shone as from some secret inner light. Bruce Kimberly was enchanted. He had not wanted to come, preferring to dine with his patients and guests at the sanatorium. He knew Ruth was disappointed and he had left with a feeling of dissatisfaction bordering on actual distress. But now he felt his spirits soar and he ate the delicious meal with keen enjoyment, all thoughts of an unpleasant nature thrust firmly into the background.

Later, in the huge, book-lined library, Mr. Tillotson became almost inquisitive regarding the sanatorium—inquiring about improvements already made and about to be made—the number of patients—or guests, as he ironically called them—"as if it was a bloomin' hostelry or roadhouse, begad. If it's a hospital, why in tunket don't you call it a hospital and be done with it?" he demanded truculently.

"But it isn't a hospital—exactly, Mr. Tillotson," Bruce explained amiably.

"No indeed, Uncle Til," Sylvia pouted. "Bruce runs a sort of glorified insane asylum. You do, too, darling!" she accused her fiancé, who had shaken his head at her.

"Far from it, sir," Bruce said hastily. "We do treat a number of mental cases, but they are not insane. Already we have discharged as cured four patients who had been suffering from neuroses of various types and severity. You see, a great many of our returned veterans need readjustment, patience and understanding and we are prepared to help them back to normal health and a new and saner outlook on life. We have been fortunate so far, and anticipate more and even more satisfactory results as we become better known. Some of our patients—or guests, if you will—are merely tired—mentally bored. They are the wealthy patients for the most part. Mrs. Botany is one and Doctor Seth Bradley another, although Doctor Bradley's condition was brought about as much from the monotony of his job as overwork. We are glad the atmosphere of Kimberly is such as to give them the rest and quiet and change they so sorely need."

"It isn't much of a place though, really, is it, darling?" Sylvia asked, darting a glance at their host. "Only a dozen or so nurses—who can't be especially efficient or they wouldn't be satisfied to work in such a remote place. Oh, I know you're completely infatuated with it, Bruce, but honestly now, isn't it something of a dump?"

Bruce got to his feet. "I resent that description of Kimberly, Sylvia," he said hotly. "It is run down. I admit that, but we have made many adjustments—some improvements and hope to make more. Our staff, however, is the best to be found anywhere. Our nurses are all registered and we are fortunate in having as technician Doctor Jefferson Thomas—you remember, sir, the man who did such fine work at the Center last year. Doctor Judson was house physician under the old regime and is a good man. I feel justified in feeling pride and deep satisfaction in our venture."

"H'm," Mr. Tillotson muttered, his deep-set eyes staring at his godchild. "But, Doctor, why do you feel your place is necessary? Westhaven is by no means a large town. The City Hospital and Medical Center are more than adequate to care for the entire county. I have heard mutterings against the place as infringing upon the work of both institutions—taking deserved profits from them. In fact, I have been approached by an interested party with a suggestion that an offer be made to buy you off—make the sanatorium an integral part of City Hospital. Now, now, you won't be the loser, Doctor," he said hastily, as Bruce showed signs of exploding. "It was suggested you be given a job—a permanent and lucrative job at the Center. How about it, boy?"

Bruce Kimberly stood for a moment, his face a mask. He was sure he had never been so angry in his life. How dared this man make such a suggestion to him? He was conscious of Sylvia's intent gaze—her almost pleading face as she watched him.

He swung to her and said stonily, "Is this some of your work, Miss Webster? Just what do you think to gain by it?" Turning back to his host he said coldly and emphatically, "My answer is no. The Kimberly Sanatorium is ours—my sister's and mine.

70

We intend making of it an institution of which some day West-haven will be proud. We have asked nothing from either the town or the county. It is solely our project and we intend it shall remain so. As for infringing on either the City Hospital or the Medical Center—that is absolutely ridiculous. Why, only a week or so ago I turned over a patient of ours to City for an operation. There is no reason why we should not work together—help each other, if you like; but Kimberly Sana-torium will never become a subsidiary of either. That is final. Now, if you will be kind enough to excuse me, I shall return to 'the dump,' as it was so inaccurately termed by Miss Web-ster." He turned and strode toward the door.

Sylvia sprang to her feet and ran to him. "Darling, darling!" she cried, two clinging hands on his arm. "Don't be like that. Uncle Till is just trying to help you—us. He is the kindest man in the world. He knows I am unhappy about you and wants to make things right for us both. Please don't be angry. Don't go."

But Bruce was not to be so easily cajoled this time. He had been deeply hurt—his pride wounded. He gently but firmly removed the clinging hands and said stiffly, "I'm sorry, Sylvia, I have to go," and shrugging into his overcoat he opened the heavy front door and let himself out into the snowy Christmas afternoon, conscious of a feeling of intense relief to be away from the place.

## 10

"WHAT'S ON YOUR mind, Doc?" Peter Allison eyed the man across the table with some concern.

Bruce shook his head, then grinned wryly. "Oh, the usual thing, Pete. Sometimes I wonder if I have been too optimistic, overambitious; if I bit off more than I can chew."

"Oh? And what brought this on, fella? From what I saw of the enterprise recently, I should say everything was progress-ing like a house afire, Ruth—your sister—is enthusiastic, al-though I think she's working much too hard. Maybe you went into it before you were quite strong enough, Doc. Perhaps Sylvia is right and you are still far from well. Could that be it, old man?"

Bruce Kimberly's eyes smoldered for a moment before he replied. "I'm all right," he said grimly, "and you don't have to tell me that Ruth is working hard. She's sold on the place —completely enamored. No, it seems there is a scheme afoot to discredit Kimberly—to take away its independence—make it a subsidiary of the Center or City Hospital. Then, to complicate things further, Doctor Morgan was in to see me last night and it seems some of the old stockholders want to get out from under—want to turn the mortgage over to First Trust and Deposit. That's Tillotson's bank, you know, and old Sam is out for my hide. Why, I can only guess. Just little things like that, Pete. Nothing important." He grinned wryly at his friend.

Peter Allison whistled softly and shoved his coffee cup back on the table. "Listen," he said earnestly. "The bank hasn't refused to accept it, has it? Of course not," Bruce shook his head again. "There is no reason why it should. That property is valuable. Of course, late years it has deteriorated and it has lost prestige. But that was all due to mismanagement, and from what I can gather everything has changed for the better and is on the up and up—since you people took over. I tell you, Doc, what you need is a business manager. You have enough to do without worrying about mortgages and things like that."

Bruce glared at his friend. "Want the job, Pete?" he began almost belligerently.

Peter Allison jumped to his feet. "I'm your man, fella. I've been dying to get my teeth into that project for years. You see, years ago my dad was one of the biggest stockholders. I used to go out there and roam about. In fact, I was almost persuaded to become a doctor myself—a psychiatrist, only I didn't call it that. Then when Dad died Doctor Morgan bamboozled Mother into selling out to him. I was away at the time but was plenty sore when I heard about it. You just leave things to your manager, old man. I'll take care of everything."

"And may I ask what compensation you expect for taking on this herculean task?" Bruce asked mockingly as he slipped into his coat.

Peter shrugged. "I know you'll insist on paying something, but honestly, I expect to get a whale of a lot of enjoyment out of working with you and Ruth—and the others, of course.

72

You know I don't need the money but—— Forget it, Bruce. You know I shall have little or nothing to do with anything except the business end of things—unless, of course, you can use me to help out at any time. I'm going to make our sanatorium famous. Wait until I get into my stride. You haven't seen anything yet. Gosh, I'm glad I'm in—at last."

Something of young Allison's enthusiasm seeped into Bruce's dark mood and as they reached the street he fell into step with his friend with more spring and buoyancy than he had felt in days. Sylvia had telephoned several times to remind him of dates he had long forgotten and could not possibly keep. She drove out to the sanatorium only to be informed that Doctor Kimberly was out of town. Ruth could give her little satisfaction and was far too busy to linger for any length of time. Sylvia, suddenly, had caught a severe cold, she said, and wanted Bruce to come see her on this particular afternoon and stay for dinner, and much against his better judgment, Bruce was on his way to the Webster mansion when Pete Allison dragged him off for a cup of coffee and a business conference at his club.

"What's the matter with Syl, Doc?" Peter asked as they parted in the parking lot. "She was all right yesterday when I saw her—except for being edgy and a bit on the quiet side. Lovers' quarrel, fella? Don't let it get you down. Sylvia needs a firm hand. I should know."

"She has a bad cold, she told me," Bruce said, a trace of doubt in his voice. "And it's none of your business——" But he said it without rancor and Peter grinned and got into his car.

Sylvia didn't look ill when Bruce reached the house. She was sitting before the fire in the library, a new novel in her listless hands. She sprang up when Bruce was announced and ran to him.

"Darling!" she cried wistfully. "Don't be mad at me. I'm sorry for what Uncle Till did to you. I didn't know. Please forgive me for even letting him say such things."

"Forget it," Bruce said gruffly, his arms, usually so warm and ardent, almost nerveless as she snuggled against him. "How did you get this cold? Want me to take your temperature? Why didn't you call your family physcian if you felt ill? I'm not the one to call, you know."

"Why not? I warned you that if I became ill I should make

73

you take care of me, darling," she reminded him. "I came out to the sanatorium and almost demanded a room, but they told me you were out of town. Where did you go, Bruce?"

"Just over to Meredith. You're not really ill, you know—just faking, aren't you? Well, I intended coming to see you anyway, so you had your trouble for nothing." He spoke levelly and moved with her to the chair she had just left. They sat down together as they had so often before, his arms about her, her golden head against his shoulder. The fire glowed and the room was filled with warm, intimate shadows. Sylvia sighed happily.

"This is so nice, darling," she murmured. "It has been so long—so very long since you were here—days and days. Don't ever be angry with me again— I—I just can't stand it."

Reminded, Bruce stiffened. "Better stop trying to manage me, Sylvia," he said somewhat shortly. "I'm not in the least manageable. And once for all understand that Kimberly Sanatorium is here to stay in spite of all your uncle may say or do to the contrary. And I, Bruce Kimberly, am and shall continue to be Chief of Staff of said Sanatorium. Get that through your lovely head and quit trying to make me into something I'm not and never could be. Now let's talk of something else."

It was well that Sylvia's face was hidden and Bruce could not see the play of emotion that marred for the moment her extraordinary beauty. The young man's arm tightened about the lovely relaxed body and the girl sighed ecstatically. The short winter afternoon merged into a stormy evening and it was almost immediately following dinner that Bruce was called back to the sanatorium. Sylvia was furious.

"It isn't fair, Bruce," she cried as the young man shrugged into his heavy coat. "You were to spend the evening with me and look what happens. I don't believe you are needed at all. They just want to keep us apart. They—— Ruth hates me." The lovely eyes swam with tears of rage and the face was flushed with resentment. Bruce stood for a moment staring at the girl before him.

"Now you're being childish—unreasonable, Sylvia," he said coldly. "How will this end? Can't you realize that my time is not my own—that I am a doctor? There can be no happiness for either of us if you insist on this insane posses-

74

siveness—this silly jealousy of my work. There are times when I wonder if you love me at all——"

"O-oh, how can you?" the girl cried stormily. "You never used to be like this—before——"

"How old are you?" the young man interrupted. "Twenty-six —seven? Twenty-five then," as the girl shook her head. "A woman. Old enough to have a certain amount of common sense. Why don't you act like a woman, my dear? I think it is you who have changed. You are not the sweet, generous girl I fell in love with."

Sylvia said nothing for a long moment while Bruce pulled on his overshoes and zipped them snugly about his ankles. Then she said stiffly, "Are you trying to tell me that you no longer love me? That there is someone else—perhaps that nurse who——"

Bruce Kimberly caught the angry girl by her slim shoulders and shook her. "Shut up!" he said grimly. "That's quite enough. When you are in a saner mood I'll see you again but not before. Good night!"

The front door closed softly and Sylvia Webster flung herself against it. Her stifled sobs were angry and she beat her fists against the polished surface in impotent fury.

"How dare he?" she demanded of the big silent house. "How dare he? Who does he think he is to talk to me so? I'll show him—I'll show them all." She went back to the library and dialed a number.

Doctor Kimberly drove into the sanatorium grounds with a feeling of relief. What ailed Sylvia? It was getting so that every time they were together there were bitter recriminations, quarrels and unpleasantness. He was getting sick of it. She could be so wonderful. She was everything he wanted—or used to be. Now he wondered. They had been engaged four years—a long time, and he supposed she had grown dissatisfied with conditions. Perhaps he should yield to her wishes for an early wedding. No doubt it was the long wait—the uncertainty that was wearing on her nerves and his, too. Somehow he didn't seem to have the patience with her moods that he used to have and perhaps marriage was the answer.

He put the car in the garage and went in the side door to

the small coatroom behind his sister's office. Voices reached him—strained and anxious. He hurried along the hall and paused before the half-open door leading into Ruth's private room. His sister looked up and saw him.

"Come in, Bruce," she called, and he noticed the relief in her voice. "Close the door, please."

"What's up?" he asked, slipping out of overcoat, gloves and galoshes. "You sound rather tragic. Oh, hello, Jill! You in this too?"

"Very much so," Jill answered anxiously.

"Let me tell him," Ruth said gently. "Doctor Bradley is gone."

"Gone! No. Why, that's impossible—fantastic," Bruce cried.

"He sent his nurse on an errand and when she returned to his rooms he just wasn't there. She thought nothing of it at first. He has been free to come and go as he saw fit; but when an hour went by and he was still absent she became concerned and began searching for him. I hesitated to call the police because of the publicity. What shall we do now? We have searched every nook and cranny in the place—the grounds, the garage and even the barns and tool sheds at the end of the lot. Not a trace. I'm worried, Bruce."

"And he said nothing about leaving—going anywhere—making a visit to someone?" he asked Jill. "Surely he couldn't go far in this weather unless dressed for it. Just what is missing from his closet?"

"His overcoat, arctics, muffler, gloves and a hat. He had talked of going in to the bank and of wanting to have another talk with a Mr. Tillotson. But the banks are all closed—have been for hours, and Mr. Tillotson has not seen him."

"Then you called Tillotson?" Bruce asked.

"Of course," his sister said. "We didn't talk with him direct but the butler told us there had been no visitors because Mr. Tillotson was suffering from an attack of influenza. Now what?"

"I want to have a look at his rooms first," the doctor said. "It isn't at all like him to do such a thoughtless thing. He should know that we would be concerned. Come along. Ordway—let's do a bit of investigating. We'll be back in a few minutes, Ruth. Don't worry. No doubt there is a perfectly logical and reasonable explanation."

They took the elevator to the third floor and along the wide corridor to the suite in the front of the building. A low humming came to their ears and as they approached, the words of an old familiar hymn reached them:

> "We are not divided,
>     All one body we,
>   One in hope and doctrine,
>       One in charity.
>   Onward——"

Jill gasped in astonishment. Bruce Kimberly turned with a paternal pat on her shoulder and retraced his steps while the girl went on into the brightly lighted sitting room where Doctor Bradley stood with his back to the fire, his chubby face wearing a benign expression.

"Were you looking for me, my dear?" he asked demurely. "Quite a stormy evening."

Jill almost gulped in her relief. "You were gone a long time, Doctor Bradley, and you know—in a way—I am responsible for your welfare and I sort of wondered if I had made a slip and—perhaps you were dissatisfied with me. You see, I didn't know. You had never done a disappearing act before."

The man laughed delightedly. "Do you know, my dear, I have always wanted to play hooky—to disappear so that I couldn't be found. Now I've done it. It was very simple and I accomplished something, I hope. Don't ask me what because I shall not tell you." He sighed almost resignedly. "My wife tells me that I'm no good at keeping a secret and maybe she's right. Have you noticed how worried our Chief has been these past few days—since Christmas, I think? Telephones are great inventions, my dear. I have had several very pleasant and satisfactory conversations with some of my most influential parishioners—with happy results I feel assured. And perhaps, also, I have been able to ease a feeling of tension here and there." He smiled, his kind eyes dancing. "Could I have something to eat—nothing at all elaborate—just whatever can be managed without fuss or bother?"

Jill stood for a long moment before she spoke. "Do you know what should be done to you, Doctor Bradley?" she said, her voice not quite steady. "You should be thoroughly spanked and put to bed without any dinner as punishment for frightening me—us almost out of our wits."

He took her hands in his, his face contrite. "I'm sorry, my dear," he said gravely. "I didn't think you would worry. After all, I am perfectly capable of taking care of myself. Would you mind explaining to me just what you thought had happened—to me—where I had gone and why?"

Jill shook her head as if to free it from anxiety. "I didn't know. I did your errand and when I returned found you gone. After an hour I became anxious. It wasn't like you and I began searching for you. When I couldn't find you I consulted Miss Kimberly. We saw your outdoor things were missing and we didn't know what to think. I came to the conclusion that I had failed you in some way and I——"

"Nonsense!" the man cried. "You are everything I want in a nurse, companion and pepper-upper. My wife spoke of adopting you and I, myself, would like nothing better. We never had a daughter—our son was killed when his plane crashed over Germany at the very beginning of the war. No, I'm sorry to have troubled you, but am glad to have set in motion a project that will ensure happiness and security to two very worthy people. Now, do I get dinner or shall I go to bed supperless?" His eyes twinkled behind his glasses and he chuckled deep in his throat. He was looking much better these last few days. The strain had left his eyes and he slept soundly at night. Mrs. Bradley seemed well pleased with his progress and had returned home much relieved.

"Please wait here, Doctor Bradley," Jill said earnestly. "I'll see what I can find in the way of food. Please don't disappear again. I just can't stand it, no matter how justifiable it may be."

As it happened, there was plenty of everything, and Jill filled a tray with appetizing food and carried it to her patient. He ate hungrily and it was while he was dining that his night nurse came on duty.

"Kind of late, aren't you, Doctor Bradley?" Marian Scott said as she waved Jill on her way, "How come?"

"That's a secret, Nurse," the man told her, finishing his

coffee. "Miss Ordway brought me a new book and I shall read quite late, so if you have anything you want to do, run along and do it. I shall be quite all right and perfectly happy."

"You're a lamb, Doctor," the girl told him, "and I wish I could take you up on that. I had an invitation to join the sleighride party tonight but of course it would come while I was on night duty. Darn it! Just my luck."

"Run along," he told her. "Honestly, I won't need you tonight. There is nothing you can do for me and I shall be quite contented right here with my book. Is Miss Ordway going on this sleighride?"

"I'll say she is—or should. Alan Blake is simply crazy about her—haunts the place hoping for a glimpse of her. Nice guy, too. Jill could do a lot worse than take him. Looks, money —everything. Some gals have all the luck, don't they, Doctor?"

"And how does Miss Ordway feel about him? I have never heard her mention him. Blake? Does he live around here?"

"Lives is right. His people own a big estate about a mile or so down the road from here. We skate on his pond—or lake; ski on his hills and in summer use his tennis courts, I suppose, and no doubt ride his horses—I hope. Alan has lots of friends. Nice chap."

"H'm'm. I see. Well, as far as I am concerned you can have the evening off and join the sleighride."

"Nothing doing, kind sir," the nurse replied. "Discipline, you know. Miss Kimberly is strict that way. Rules are rules and there is no deviating from the straight and narrow in Kimberly. No, sir. But read your book and I'll be around if you need me for anything." She picked up the tray and departed and if she was disappointed at missing the sleighride it didn't show too plainly in her serene face and quick step. That was one of the things Doctor Bradley admired in these girls. No grousing.

Quiet settled in the pleasant sitting room of Doctor Bradley's suite. The fire crackled cheerily while outside the snow drifted as the wind swirled it into mounds and furrows and piled it against the window sills. For a moment he thought of the crowd of young people starting out on a sleighride in this storm. But youth knew no fear and the very fury of the elements would merely prove a challenge. He sighed unconsciously, his thoughts shifting to his son, that intrepid boy

**79**

whose life had ended almost before it began. He could see him now—waving as his plane mounted higher and higher to be at last lost in infinity. Always young—that was it. Nick would be always young. He picked up his book and began to read and was soon lost to everything but the tale that unfolded before him.

11

"Is ANYTHING THE matter, Jill?" Alan Blake asked as the sleighing party got under way. "You are very quiet—even for you."

"Just tired, I guess," Jill answered, making an effort to shake off the depression that had taken possession of her earlier in the day.

He slipped his arm along the back of the seat behind Jill and she relaxed against it. Why not? Alan was a dear—giving so much and demanding nothing in return—just to be with her occasionally—grateful for the casual friendliness she gave.

"How are things going at the sanatorium these days, Jill?" he asked after a moment. "Seems to me I heard something about closing up the place. I certainly hope it's not true."

Jill stiffened and sat erect, resisting Alan's attempt to draw her back against his arm. "I don't know how such stories get started," she said coldly. "There isn't a grain of truth in it —I happen to know."

"Sorry," the young man murmured. "Sylvia Webster met my sister at a cocktail party the other day and happened to mention it. Syl's engaged to Kimberly, isn't she? Or she was. Sis thought all was not quite smooth in that quarter. They've been engaged for ages—maybe the affection of each is wearing thin. Could be, you know. Well, no long engagement for me—when the time comes. I'll just grab the gal and beat it for the nearest preacher or Justice of the Peace." He laughed and Jill relaxed again. "I sound like a gossipy old hen, Jill," he told her.

This was just conversation, Jill told herself. She took no stock in any of it, either the yarn about the sanatorium or the rift between Kim and Sylvia Webster. There wasn't a chance she would ever let him go.

The others were singing and Alan joined them, his fine baritone distinctive amid the jangle of voices. Jill hummed softly to herself, then she, too, let her voice out and was surprised to find that she and Alan were actually singing a duet—the others were silent or humming a low accompaniment. She stopped abruptly.

"What's the matter?" she demanded. "Why did you stop? It's so lovely when everyone sings." So once again their united voices rang out on the cold winter air.

They stopped at a farmhouse several miles from town and ate oyster stew with fresh, crusty rolls, baked ham and sweet potatoes, crisp green salad, apple pie and coffee. And because Jill had not eaten her usual dinner before starting out, she enjoyed every mouthful of the delicious meal. The farmer and his wife, with two women from neighboring farms, served and laughed and chatted companionably. After the meal the party adjourned to the spacious living room where they played childish games: spin the platter, blind man's buff, charades and other old-fashioned, long forgotten games. Jill was having a very good time. Ann Burke and Jeff were the life of the party and Jill laughed more than she had in months. Someone discovered a mouth organ, someone else a comb and Ann and Jeff did a cake walk—bending and twisting, whirling and spinning like automatons. Jeff clowned in imitations—from an opera singer to that of a soprano rendering an anthem in a choir. It was very funny. Jeff was a revelation to Jill.

The grandfather's clock in the hall struck ten and Jill suddenly sobered. "We must be going back, Alan," she said softly. "Ann and I have to be in by eleven. I hate to break this up but we live by rule at the sanatorium, you know."

"Okay," the young man answered and got to his feet. "Come on, kids," he shouted above the din. "Time to go back. Get your wraps and we'll rout Tony out of his snug berth in the kitchen." He left the room and the others found coats and caps, galoshes and mittens and gathered in the wide hall.

"It was a lovely party, Mrs. Wales," Jill told the plump hostess who stood just inside the kitchen door watching the others. "I think I never had a better time in my life. It was

81

such fun and the dinner was delicious. Thank you so very much." Her hand, warm and friendly, pressed that of the farmer's wife and the woman beamed on her.

The sleigh seemed a long time reaching the front door and Jill wondered if something had happened. She knew the storm had increased in fury during the last two hours but there had not been a great deal of snow in the highway when they came out. It was a relief when she heard the faint jingle of sleigh-bells and the loud "whoa" as the driver halted the team before the farm door.

"Gosh!" Alan cried as the snow rushed into the hall. "A blizzard! Come on, you kids—pile out before we freeze these people." Laughing and shouting they floundered through a huge drift several feet deep and fell panting and gasping into the sleigh. The horses snorted and pawed the loose snow, their breath a cloud of steam in the cold night air.

"Hope we make it all right," the driver growled as the big sleigh moved heavily forward. "Might better've stayed at the Waleses' till mornin'. No sense riskin' life an' limb tryin' to get through these drifts t'night. It's dark as blazes, too."

"The horses will keep to the road, Tony. I'm sure you've been out on worse nights than this."

"Not lately, I ain't," the man grumbled. " 'Tain't fit fer men nor beast."

"Want me to drive?" Alan asked, pressing Jill's hand in his.

"Oh, I guess I can manage—fer a spell anyways," Tony answered, grumpily.

"Then suppose you stop grousing. It isn't like you—that's why I had you drive us tonight. Cheer up, we're doing fine."

A grunt was Tony's answer and he shouted to the horses who were making valiant efforts to buck each new drift as they came to it.

"Hope we don't tip over," was the next cheerful suggestion of the driver as the big sleigh swerved.

Jill laughed and Alan said, "Don't mind him, Jill. He's merely raising the ante. It will undoubtedly cost me an extra ten-spot before we get back. But it was worth it—if you enjoyed the party, Jill. Have you?"

"I loved every minute of it, Alan," Jill told him. "It's the first sleighride party I've been to in years—since I came East to train, for that matter. We used to have them often back home."

"How about coming on a twosome some afternoon?" he asked, while Ann and Jeff, snuggled close beneath a fur robe, strained their ears to listen.

"Make it a foursome and sold, Alan," Jeff said. "Haven't you got a two-seater? We could do some skiing in those intriguing hills after this storm—or couldn't we?"

"Dangerous!" volunteered Tony, clucking to the horses who had met a particularly heavy drift. "Git up there—ain't got all night!" he shouted at the laboring team. "Man got killed couple years back—broke his fool neck."

"What makes you so cheerful tonight, Tony?" Alan wanted to know, joining the laughter of the others.

"I bet I know," shouted a little blonde neighbor of Alan's. "They had just opened a jug of cider when you dragged him away, Al. And he's sweet on Phoebe Case, the plump, black-eyed gal who waited on table. Didn't you notice that she kept ʌing back to the kitchen? Don't you care, Tony—I think she ̣kes you in spite of your grouches."

"Oh, you go on!" Tony muttered, chirruping to the team, · he grinned sheepishly and from then on had no more dire predictions. Jill, Ann and Jeff were the last to leave the sleigh and Alan reiterated his invitation for an afternoon sleighride.

"Be sure to make it on our afternoon off duty," Ann reminded him. "It's seldom we three are off at the same time like tonight, but perhaps we will be able to work it by switching with someone else. Thanks for the swell party, Alan. Good night!"

Jeff Thomas wallowed through the heavy drifts to his own apartment and stood for a moment on the deep porch shaking off the snow. It had been a pleasant interlude and he was glad he had gone. Bruce should have been along, too. He needed just such relaxation. That was the matter with him— too tense—too wrapped up in this place. He hoped there was no truth in the rumor Blake had reported. He knew something was in the wind—that Bruce was troubled, but it was one of those things an outsider had better keep out of. He had a little money if Bruce needed it. He had even broached the subject the day before yesterday only to have Doc inform him he didn't need it and wouldn't take it if he did. It had sounded almost brusque; but the warm handclasp took away the sting.

Both Bruce and Ruth knew he would do anything for either of them. He gave himself a final shake and let himself into the dimly lighted hall. Eleven o'clock. He released the night latch, snapped off the light and went upstairs to his small apartment.

Over in the nurses' home Ann sat down on Jill's bed for a last-minute chat. "Isn't Alan Blake a prince, Jill?" Ann asked, eyeing the other quizzically. "I believe the lug sort of likes you—sort of, don't you?"

"Does he? Well, I like him—a lot," Jill replied imperturbably. "They were all fine people—even Tony." She laughed softly.

"Did you know the Chief didn't approve of our going, Jill? Miss Kimberly was nervous. She thought the storm might prove serious and her big brother called the whole thing a crazy stunt. Jealous, I bet a dollar—because he wasn't invited. Dog in the manger."

"Oh, I don't think so," Jill said. "He probably knows th country in this part of the state and I can think of pleasanter situations than being stuck in a snowbank on a night like this —miles from anywhere."

"Pooh!" scoffed Ann. "Don't you suppose Alan Blake knows this country around here, too? Do you think, for one minute, that he would have risked marooning us? Of course not. Anyway, it was fun and I had a grand time. I guess you did, too, didn't you?" she asked, yawning widely and getting up from the bed. "I'm dead on my feet. 'Night, darling. See you in the morning—I hope."

Jill undressed slowly. It had been a pleasant interval, She was glad she had gone. She went to the window and opened it, slipping a winter screen into place. There was a light in the Kimberly living room and even as she watched it went out. She slipped into bed and pulled the blankets snugly about her shoulders. But sleep didn't come immediately. What was it Alan had said about there being a rift in the affair between Kim and Sylvia Webster? Was that the reason for his worried look? Doctor Bradley had noticed it and—had he tried to straighten it out—to patch up the differences—if any? But of course that was fantastic. No girl having been blessed with his love would do anything to risk losing it. It was unthinkable. Of course, it had been a long engagement and she had often wondered why they didn't marry. What were they waiting for? She frowned and burrowed deeper into her pillow, and at last she slept.

And over in the Kimberly living room, Bruce put aside the paper he had been reading and listened to the storm raging outside. Blake was a fool to risk a sleighride on a night like this. He recalled a story that only a couple of years back a group of youngsters had been marooned for hours back in the hills and when the snowplow dug them out next morning there were several cases of frostbite and plenty of colds. He wished he had forbidden any of his staff being a party to any such crazy scheme. Forbid? How could he? It was Ruth who made the rules in this place and she had scoffed at his fears—calling him an old granny. But just the same, here it was nearly eleven and they weren't back. Jeff Thomas should have had more sense even if the girls lacked it. He rose and walked to the window. Snow swirled and eddied in the gale. The world was white—the surface unbroken. The busses had stopped hours ago and no snowplow had been through—probably wouldn't be until daylight.

Was that the sound of sleighbells? He listened intently. It was coming down the road—laughter and sleighbells—shouts, then three shadows wallowing through drifts to the porch of the nurses' home. He sighed in relief. The clock in the hall boomed eleven and he returned to his chair before the dying fire. Somehow he felt old tonight—old and out of everything. He hadn't been on a sleighride in years. It might be fun. For a moment he felt exhilarated, then he slumped. Sylvia couldn't abide sleighrides. She preferred the family limousine or her own closed car. What was happening to him and Sylvia? What had become of the ecstasy which had filled him at the mere thought of his fiancée? He shook himself and got to his feet. The fire was nearly out. He placed the screen in front of the grate and turned off the reading light. Suddenly he was very tired and mounted the stairs to his room slowly, a step at a time.

Over in the sanatorium Doctor Bradley put down his book. The fire was reduced to a few last glowing embers. His night nurse came into the room.

"It's nearly eleven, Doctor. Time you were asleep. Anything I can get you? A nightcap—oh, of course I mean hot milk or something of the sort?"

The doctor shook his head. "Nothing, thank you. It has been a pleasant evening, Nurse. A bright fire, an interesting book, a comfortable chair and quiet. You are very understanding, my dear," he went on. "I am indeed fortunate in having two such considerate and charming companions. I think, however, I shall retire now. I heard the sleighride party return a few minutes ago. Did you?"

"Who could help it?" the nurse laughed. "Sleighbells aren't common in this day and age. I bet they had a grand time." She went into the bedroom and turned down the bed, laying out slippers and warm robe. The doctor was standing at the window when she came back. He turned as she entered.

"A bad night. I'm glad they returned safely. Good night, my dear."

He walked quickly into the next room and Marian Scott went about the room touching an article here and there and thinking of the party she had missed.

In the library of the Webster mansion, Sylvia Webster sat before the telephone talking—demanding, pleading, cajoling and at last crying triumphantly, "You will! Oh, you are such lambs!" She too ran to the tall window and pulled aside the heavy curtain. She shivered. "It will clear tomorrow," she said aloud. "They can make it all right. They have got to make it." She dropped the curtain and ran up the stairs to her room where a sleepy maid was waiting.

12

"BUSY?" PETER ALLISON asked from the door of Doctor Kimberly's office.

"No more than usual," Bruce replied. "What's on your mind, Pete? Come on in and make yourself comfortable."

"Perhaps Ruth should be in on this, too; but somehow I wanted you to hear it first."

"Okay. Shoot!" Doctor Kimberly laid down an unopened

letter and the thin blade on top of it, then leaned back in his chair.

"What do you think of the endowment idea, Doc?"

Bruce stared. "I don't think I quite know what you mean, Pete. What endowment?"

"Well, it seems there are five wealthy men desirous of making some sort of permanent recognition—in fact a gesture of thanksgiving or a sort of memorial as the case might be——"

"Just what are you trying to say, Pete? I don't understand."

"Listen. In words of one or two syllables—five men all bearing scars, though not physical, from the late war, want to pool a certain amount—one hundred thousand to be specific—and endow Kimberly Sanatorium. One man lost a son, the only son of another was badly maimed but came back, the wife of one headed a nursing unit overseas somewhere and saw plenty of action, and sons of the other two men got off scot free. All five are millionaires and are anxious to help any mentally injured or lost veterans wherever possible. They like what they have heard of Kimberly, Doc, and have decided to endow us. What do you think of the proposition?"

"Endow Kimberly, Pete? How on earth did they ever hear about us? We are so new! We are small and still struggling along, experimenting, and while we have had some success——"

"I don't think I am betraying any confidence, but you have friends, you know. Your patients like you and adore Ruth. This place is different from the average sanatorium. You must know that. There's a hominess here—a feeling of health—that raises a patient's morale. Well, what do you think?"

Bruce shook his head. "I don't know what to think, Pete. We haven't room for many more patients. The mortgage is large and I suspect for a few years we shall do little more than break even, financially. Who are these men? Local people? Do they know Kimberly Sanatorium? Have they seen it—looked over the property and its possibilities? And just why should they choose us, Pete? Are you back of this project?"

Pete shook his head. "I was as surprised as you are," he told him. "Without permission I can't tell you the name of the person who suggested the idea to these five men. But I can say this much. None of the donors live in this section of the country and the instigator is an admiring patient. I believe the patient —or perhaps I should say ex-patient—stands so high in the estimation, for wisdom, integrity and real goodness, of all five prospective donors, that the reaction was instantaneous— without question. As your business manager I suggest you accept the offer—with thanks. The interest, while not excessive, will give you a chance to make part of the improvements you planned—enlarging, perhaps, or increasing your personnel and equipment. Talk it over with Ruth, Doc, and let me know as soon as you can. We want to get this thing buttoned up—and fast."

"What did you do about the mortgage, Pete?" Bruce asked worriedly. "I was going to ask about that before but had so many things on my mind it became sidetracked. Do these men know about the mortgage?"

"I couldn't say," Pete answered. "No one asked me and I didn't volunteer the information. Anyway, the mortgage is taken care of—all sewed up snug and tight and you have nothing to worry about in that quarter. The lawyers for the investors will receive the interest payments semi-annually and won't crowd you for the principal. It should give you a swell feeling of accomplishment," he went on, "to know that five men— strangers—think enough of your efforts and ideas to want to sink one hundred thousand dollars in your sanatorium—to invest that much money as a sort of memorial or thank offering, as the case might be, on the strength of what you stand for. I think it's grand and am proud to be associated with you and it. There, fella, I've got that off my chest and will get back to work."

After the door closed upon his business manager, Bruce Kimberly sat for a long time, his mind in a turmoil. Who was responsible for this idea? It seemed fantastic. What had he done to warrant it? For a moment he knew a feeling of apprehension—suspicion. Was it possible that Tillotson was behind this? He shook his head. No, not hard-headed, tight-fisted Sam Tillotson—not the Websters either. Anyway, Pete had said the men were not from this section. He dropped his head in his hands and it was so that his sister found him when she entered the room a few minutes later.

"What's the matter, Bruce?" she asked in concern. "Headache? Or is the mail less pleasant than usual?"

"Sit down," he said, shaking his head as if to dispel the uneasiness. "I have just received a shock, Ruth, and I can't seem to assimilate the facts."

"Shock?" his sister repeated. "Tell me."

"Somewhere in this wide country of ours are five men—millionaires all. All bear some mark of the late war. They want to erect or endow some sort of memorial or thank offering, as the case might be, something in the nature of assured and continued aid to veterans who have lost their bearings and might need help."

"But we have veterans' hospitals, Bruce," Ruth pointed out. "They are scattered all through the country. How does that affect us?"

"They chose Kimberly as the beneficiary of their one hundred thousand dollar endowment."

"Wh-at?"

"They picked Kimberly Sanatorium, Ruth, because of what they have heard of us—because of the good reports coming to them of our treatment and its results. Of our home-in-a-sanatorium idea."

"But who—why—what?"

"That's what I don't know. Pete just told me about it. Some patient—man or woman he didn't specify, although I have an idea it must be a man; most of our patients—all of our veterans have been men—took it upon himself to father the scheme and all five donors fell for it wholeheartedly, from all accounts. They must certainly have had implicit faith in his sound judgment." He shook his head again. "What do you think of it, Ruth?"

Ruth's eyes were shining with excitement. "Why—why—I think it's wonderful—magnificent—stupendous! What we can't do with that money, darling! Pfft! *That* for the mortgage, Bruce, and with the rest we can remodel and enlarge and beautify to our heart's content. O-h! I'm so thrilled!"

Bruce laughed ruefully. "It's only the interest we can use, Ruth," he pointed out, "and that isn't so much, although it will help considerably. It will give us a chance to lower our rates—even accept a few non-paying patients."

"Of course," Ruth cried happily. "Stupid of me not to realize we couldn't use it all; but just the same, it's going to help a lot. But tell me, Bruce, why pick on us? We're new, practically, and untried in a way. Of course I know the cures have happened to be somewhat spectacular—at least two or three have—but there must be any number of better known, larger and finer sanatoriums they could have chosen."

"That's what puzzles me. Pete could tell me very little. He's the business manager, he informed me, and advised our accepting at once and begin planning on expansion and improvements. But do you know, it sort of scares me, Ruth. It will be a great responsibility. More will be expected of us. We shall have to increase our staff—add another doctor, perhaps, and several nurses, and you know how hard that is going to be. Oh, well, Pete is pretty level-headed and I imagine he knows what he's doing."

"You don't suppose he's at the bottom of it? He is very rich, I know, and——"

"But he was never a patient here, Ruth," her brother pointed out. "At least not while we've been here. And that has been scarcely five months." He shook his head. "Things are moving too fast for me," he said.

"I'm going in to have a talk with Mr. Peter Allison, Bruce," Ruth said. "Maybe I can squeeze a little more information out of him. Have you heard how he came out regarding the mortgage? No? Nor have I," she said as her brother's head moved from side to side almost resignedly and she prepared to leave the room, "but I intend finding out—I hope."

Peter Allison was talking on the telephone when Ruth knocked on his door. She waited a minute until she heard him say, "Wait, please. Someone at my door." She went in and he motioned her to a seat and went on with his conversation, his side of which confined itself to "Yes. No. I see. I'll let you know. Good-bye." He cradled the instrument and turned to his visitor.

"Did I interrupt anything important, Pete?" Ruth asked.

"All my telephone conversations are important, beautiful," he told her. "What can I do for you?"

"Bruce has been telling me a fantastic story about five men who wish to endow Kimberly Sanatorium. He says you know all about it. If you do, I wish you would tell me. I can't seem to quite take it in. Just why this sudden interest in Kimberly, Pete? And just who may these altruists be?"

"I explained everything I was at liberty to divulge to Doc,

90

Ruth. After all, while I may be your business manager and in that capacity receive all sorts of suggestions and make some necessary contacts and commitments, yet I don't have to broadcast details or confidences even to you, my bosses—or more especially to you. So, my dear, you just leave everything to me. I know what I'm doing and your affairs are perfectly safe in my hands. You do trust me, don't you? Implicitly? Good!" as Ruth nodded, somewhat reluctantly however.

"Of course, Pete. We both think you're wonderful even if you can be most aggravating at times," she told him getting slowly to her feet. "And there are times when I wonder just why you are doing all this. What you expect to get out of it."

"You'd be surprised if I should tell you—now, darling," the young man said. "But I can tell you this. I'm getting a big kick out of everything right this minute but some day I shall present my bill. Oh, don't worry, it won't be beyond your ability to pay, I hope. In the meantime don't worry about a thing. Leave everything to Pete. He'll manage."

Ruth Kimberly bit her lip. "All right for you," she said childishly. "I think you're mean."

He swung around in his chair. "What did you decide— you and Doc?"

"I have a notion not to tell you. Two can play at that game. But it is all so wonderful—so unbelievable and story-bookish that I can't understand how I came to swallow it, hook, line and sinker and so painlessly, too. If I should wake up and find it all just a dream or a silly hoax, I think I should never forgive you, Peter Allison."

"It's neither a dream nor a hoax, Ruth," Pete said seriously. "I was just as amazed and doubtful as you are. However, I now know the entire project is sincere and aboveboard. Run along, gal; you confuse me and I have things to do—important things. Don't forget our date for Friday night. I'm counting on it."

"Don't!" Ruth snapped as she closed the door.

Pete grinned to himself as he picked up the telephone. "But I shall, darling," he said aloud then gave a number to the impatient operator.

Ruth climbed the stairs to Rodney Kent's room. Mary Blanchard met her at the door.

91

"No change," she said in answer to the look of inquiry on the superintendent's face.

The patient lay on his back, his dark eyes closed, or nearly closed. Sometimes the nurse had an idea he was watching her with sinister motives, but she said nothing about it to anyone except to the night nurse, Jill Ordway, who had smiled at the other's small shiver of apprehension. Jill had acknowledged that she, herself, thought he sensed more than they realized and said as much to Doctor Kimberly who agreed with her. Bruce Kimberly didn't feel any too easy about Rodney Kent. He had hesitated before accepting him for treatment when his father had broached the subject ten days before.

"But listen, Doctor," the older man had pleaded. "You have helped others—you can't refuse trying to help my son. I know something of what you did for young Woodworth and the Blackmore boy. And there are others who speak highly of your work here. I want you to admit my son—give him the benefit of your treatment. If, after two weeks, you see no least sign of improvement I promise to take him away—move him on to Minnesota; but that is the final recourse—there's nothing after that for him—or for me. I am willing to pay anything, Doctor. Will you do it?"

So against his better judgment Bruce Kimberly gave his consent, and Rodney Kent, scion of vast wealth, a young man who in health had boasted an unbridled passion and during the war had broken more rules and regulations than any other man in Uncle Sam's army yet somehow managed to get by uncensured and unscathed, was laid low from some mysterious malady that kept him in a state of coma, his huge body and agile brain dormant. Jeff Thomas had given him several shocks, but electric and heat therapy seemed to have little or no effect on his condition.

Now Ruth Kimberly looked down at the big young man with something almost maternal in her fine eyes. She brushed back the heavy hair from his forehead and murmured softly: "Why don't you wake up, laddie? You are missing a great deal of fun and worthwhile things. Is it that you are tired or lazy or just don't care that your father is frantic with worry?" Her hand slipped to his pulse which was slow and regular. "Do you know, Rodney Kent," she went on quietly, "I can't believe there is much the matter with you. X-rays show no pressure anywhere. I think it is about time you came to yourself. Do you know it?"

Mary Blanchard stared curiously as the superintendent carried on this low-voiced, one-sided conversation and Miss Kimberly smiled as she saw the strange look in the nurse's face.

"I have found that sometimes a word or two gets through to the subconscious in cases such as this, Blanchard," she explained. "It is always worth trying." She examined his chart and went out.

She passed Mrs. Botany's door and stopped for a moment to chat with the inquisitive old lady.

"How are things going, Ruth?" Mrs. Botany demanded. She had long since given over addressing the superintendent as Miss Kimberly. In fact, the only persons on the staff who were not called by his or her first name were the Chief-of-Staff and Doctor Judson. The latter was always called "Judson," never Doctor Judson. She knew it annoyed him and was enormously pleased because it did. She seemed to stand somewhat in awe of Bruce, however, and except when speaking of him to his sister when he was "your brother," he was always Doctor Kimberly.

"Very well, Mrs. Botany," Ruth said. "In fact, very well indeed. The Kimberly fairy godmothers have taken a hand in our affairs at long last and things are looking up. Don't be surprised to see another doctor on the staff one of these days and several more nurses—if we can get them. We expect to add a wing or two and we may even come to the point of hiring a secretary for my brother, which last is to me the very acme of success—the final expression of luxury."

"Humph!" trumpeted the old woman. "Someone left you a fortune? If they have don't sink it in this place. Sell out and spend it having a good time. You're young—get away from this house of pain and doldrums."

Ruth shook her head. "Not us, my dear. This is our life. We love it and whatever money we get is going into it so that it will be better equipped to bring health and happiness to the poor souls who, for a brief space, have lost their way. I'm wondering if you wouldn't enjoy helping, Mrs. Botany."

"What is this, a holdup, Ruth Kimberly?" the old woman demanded indignantly. "No siree, I'm not paying one cent more than I agreed to. You won't give me the nurse I want

93

so why should I spend my money so that someone else can have her? I suppose Peter Allison has been up to some of his shenanigans again. I declare I don't know what is to become of him. Why don't you marry him, Ruth, and teach him sense —though to tell the truth I'm not so sure you've got any to spare yourself. What you blushing for, girl? Like him, don't you? Well then, get busy. I'm tired. Send that dratted Halstead girl to me. I sent her packing with a bug in her ear a few minutes ago. I suppose she's sulking. I dislike people who sulk and you can tell her so. Good-bye."

Ruth patted the thin, blue-veined hand impatiently tapping the arm of her chair and said softly, "You're an old humbug. You haven't a mean bone in your body and you know it. I wish we could let you have Jill Ordway, but she is on a very special case just now."

"Humph!" the old woman snorted. "A preacher! What's so special about him that he has to have my nurse?"

"Ah, but she is not with Doctor Bradley just now, Mrs. Botany," Ruth explained. "She is on night duty in 69—the Kent boy—you know, the down-east Kents. His father brought him here because our treatment of similar cases has proven successful. He has been here more than a week now."

"Well?"

Ruth shook her head. "No change that we can see. Both Doctor Kimberly and Doctor Thomas have the idea he will snap out of his comatose state suddenly and they are probably right. He's a huge young man—went through the war without a scratch and then to come to this. It is very sad."

"Kent? Rodney Kent? I remember a Kent child who was a brat if ever there was one. The family visited in my neighborhood when I lived on the Cape. Probably the same brat grown bigger and worse. And so he gets my nurse. Bah! No justice even here. Good-bye!"

Ruth laughed softly. "We put Jill on the case because she has had experience in such cases and is really quite wonderful with neurotic patients."

"So that's it, is it? I suppose if I should be loony you'd manage to give me the nurse I want. Is that it? Rubbish! Good-bye! I mean it."

"All right, my dear. Good-bye, and I feel sure it wasn't you

94

who wanted us to have all that money. But thank you just the same. Good-bye!"

"You come back here, Ruth Kimberly!" the old woman cried, but Ruth waved her hand and left.

So is wasn't Mrs. Botany. She might try Doctor Bradley, but of course it wasn't at all likely he knew anything about it. From her own experience she knew that clergymen never had too much money and if they could lay their hands on any appreciable amount it went right back into the church and its work. She shook her head. No doubt of it, Peter Allison was surely up to his old shenanigans as his godmother had said. How else to explain it?

### 13

"So Sylvia is visiting in New York," Ruth Kimberly said to her brother one Sunday morning as they ate a leisurely breakfast. "Did you see this, Bruce?" she asked, handing the morning paper across the table to him. "Did you know she was going?"

Bruce shook his head, his mouth full of toast. He swallowed and took the paper, folded to show an excellent cut of his fiancée with King, who appeared to have grown even bigger. His pulse quickened as he gazed at the lovely face. How beauful she was!

"I am ashamed to say that I haven't seen her very lately, Ruth," he said regretfully.

"Why? Haven't things been going well between you, Bruce?"

"Not too well," he replied morosely. "Of course it has been my fault, Ruth, and I have about made up my mind to forget my foolish pride and consent to an immediate marriage. Probably that has been the whole trouble between us. Long engagements have a way of playing havoc with one's nerves. We have quarreled—no, not quarreled exactly; but whenever we are together she's jittery and says things she doesn't mean and that I resent. Marriage may be the answer. I don't know."

"And you a psychiatrist! Shame on you! More toast, dear?

Bacon? Coffee, then? Sure you will have nothing more? All right, Margaret," she called to the housekeeper, "Doctor Kimberly and I will not be over for lunch but expect to be here for dinner. Have it a bit early tonight, will you? Say—six-thirty? Good!"

They set out for the sanatorium, walking briskly along the freshly shoveled path on the crisp late February morning, breathing deeply of the cold invigorating air. Ruth gazed upon the big sprawling building with deep affection not unmixed with pride.

"Don't you love it, Bruce?" she asked. "Even though I can see its many imperfections—see a great deal to be done—so much of very necessary work needed to make it into what we want, yet there is something heartwarming about it. It seems to represent the promise of a dream fulfilled—of a goal reached—an ideal for which we are both striving. It is all very clear in my own mind, Bruce, although I describe it badly. This is what I trained for——"

"I know," her brother murmured, his critical gaze on the sanatorium—seeing all his sister saw and more. Smoke curled lazily upward from the huge chimneys. Early morning sunlight made dazzling jewels of the myriad windows. Two of the outdoor men were clearing snow from the driveway and front walk, carrying on a desultory conversation as they labored. Sara, one of the maids, came from the back door to scatter crumbs to birds waiting in the low bushes at the rear of the building. Somewhere a window opened for a brief moment and curtains billowed in the light wind. Ruth called a gay good morning to the shovelers, who touched caps and stood watching for a moment. Bruce lifted a hand in greeting and was answered in like manner. Yes, he said to himself, it was a good morning—a good life.

"I have a feeling this is just the beginning, Bruce," Ruth said happily. "I have a notion our lean days are over. We have passed the crisis and are now on the up and up, as Peter would say. I am so very glad for you, darling. It sort of compensates——"

"For surgery, Ruth?" he asked wryly. "It helps," he said. He caught her hand and together they ran up the steps to the front door.

"Not only your career in surgery," Ruth said to herself as

she removed her wraps, "but for all the things you are beginning to discover your blonde sweetheart is not. I hope and pray the rift will widen beyond all chance of bridging. Sylvia Webster is not worth your little finger, my dear brother, and it is about time you found it out." She tucked a recalcitrant curl in place before her narrow office mirror. "I hope you remain in New York—forever!" she muttered, then thrust all thought of Sylvia Webster from her mind and started on the day's round of duties.

There was a new patient in room 45—Doctor Bronson Reynolds, Ph.D., late headmaster of an ultra select boys' school. He was not a young man and had been a sufferer from arthritis several years. Lately he had become a hypochondriac and his worried family hoped the treatment used at Kimberly might effect a cure. In the few days he had been here, he had developed a series of other complaints which he described at length to anyone who would listen. His voice was trying—thin and whining, at variance with his appearance. He complained of "something" in his stomach that snatched up everything he ate, so that he didn't get anything at all. He complained that the air he breathed went into his lungs and then leaked out before he had a chance to exhale, and to prove it he would pant in short, labored gasps. He argued that his brain was swelling and pushing outward so that his head always felt heavy. His eyes were blank—his expression constantly worried. He was easily excited and at any loud noise or sudden movement would start and immediately have a dizzy spell. He sometimes talked of suicide as the best way out.

His day nurse was the calm, serene but husky Beulah Wyman who soothed and babied him out of his darkest moods but had difficulty in making him eat his meals. He would shake his head and turn away.

"Got to starve that *thing* in my stomach, Nurse," he would explain. "It's the only way."

"If he doesn't eat his food, what becomes of it?" his night nurse wanted to know when she heard of his refusal to eat. "His tray goes back to the kitchen clean as a whistle—at least that's what they tell me. Imagination, probably, and yet the man looks half-starved."

His day nurse shook her head. "He is slowly starving himself. He has been here three days now and I understand there's to be a change in treatment. The poor fellow thinks and talks of nothing but himself. He's an exaggerated introvert. I suppose it's an escape from his world of learning—teaching—governing. I feel dreadfully sorry for him."

"Sounds to me like involutional melancholia," the night nurse said ruefully. "I don't care for that type. They require close watching. Do you know, Wyman, I'm none too keen about this case."

"Don't be silly," Wyman said. "There's nothing to be afraid of. I agree with Miss Kimberly. She's a great believer in occupational therapy and this morning we are going to try to interest him in modeling. He has beautiful hands. Have you noticed?"

The other nodded. "Oh, he's not a bad-looking guy, but just the same——" She shrugged. "Well, here's wishing you luck, Wyman," she said and left.

It was soon after that the superintendent arrived bringing with her a quantity of modeling clay but no tools. Better have them come later if the patient showed signs of being interested. The nurse raised the head of the bed and Ruth Kimberly drew a chair close and placed the tray across the patient's knees.

"Have you ever done any modeling, Doctor Reynolds?" she asked. "We are planning various changes here at Kimberly and I should like a number of figurines—man or beast—fish or fowl, whatever you like. I learned a little modeling in college and found it great fun." All the time she was talking her hands were busy and the man watched her, at first listlessly, then almost eagerly. "There!" she exclaimed triumphantly as she set the tiny cat on the tray. "Do you recognize it?"

"C-a-t," the patient murmured. "But no whiskers. Whoever heard of a cat without whiskers?" His hands were at the clay —molding it almost absently and the two nurses watched. At last he set what he declared was a deer beside the cat. He looked at it proudly, then turned an inquiring glance on his audience.

"Not bad," the superintendent told him, "not bad at all for a first attempt. I wish you could make me a flock of wild geese —in relief, of course; but perhaps that is too difficult for you. Then there are flowers, babies, Indian heads—oh, a great many things. I'm sure if you will keep at it I shall have my geese."

"How big do you want it, Miss Kimberly?" the man asked in a voice neither of the women had ever heard before—quiet, cultured and controlled. "If I knew that I could plan and think about it—nights when I can't sleep." His voice changed abruptly to the thin whine his associates found so trying. "You know, when my head swells so big I think it will burst." He turned to the wall, his face tragic.

Ruth Kimberly removed the tray and his nurse lowered the bed. "Time for your nap, Doctor Reynolds," Wyman told him cheerily, wiping the clay from his hands and smoothing the blankets across his shoulders. The superintendent seemed pleased with the small success that had been accomplished.

"No more unless he asks for it, Wyman," she said as she prepared to leave the room. "If this fails we shall try something else; but I feel sure he is definitely interested."

"I do too," the nurse agreed. "I was watching his eyes. They were alive for the first time."

"It will be slow going—but well worth it if it works," Miss Kimberly said as she closed the door.

She encountered Doctor Bradley on the stairs and the two paused for a brief chat. His nurse waited below. She looked very pretty this morning.

"Going for a walk, Doctor?" Ruth asked the clergyman. "Ending in church, of course. I wish I could go with you. It's such a grand morning—cold yet invigorating. One thing about our climate here that's in our favor is its dryness. I suppose because we are so high. Don't walk too far, Reade, and be sure you are dressed warmly."

"I'm all right," Ellen Reade laughed, "and I'm sure my patient is, too. We'll walk only part way, Miss Kimberly, and take the bus at Martin's. We're both warm-blooded and vigorous, aren't we, Doctor?"

"You are, I'm sure," he told her, "and I like to think I am, also. How are things shaping up, my dear?" he asked the superintendent.

"Wonderfully, Doctor. Sometime I shall pay you a social call and tell you all about it."

"I shall enjoy that," the doctor told her, "and I, too, wish you were coming with us," he added as he joined his companion. Ruth Kimberly went on down the stairs to her brother's office.

Bruce was not in his office and she stood for a moment looking out at the glittering, snow-covered world. She recalled the conversation at breakfast and wondered just how wide was the rift between her brother and Sylvia Webster. Bruce had changed since returning from overseas; but then most returned veterans were different, and why not? Some of them had been mere boys in their teens when the war began and their terrible experiences had sobered and aged them far more than the added years warranted. Bruce, while no longer a boy in years, had kept most of his endearing boyish traits up until the time of his enlistment. Now he was a man, and sometimes, Ruth felt, no longer a very *young* man. It was not due alone to his harrowing experience as an army surgeon in battle-torn North Africa, but to the subsequent nerve exhaustion and tragic loss of his career as well. She had hoped and was still hoping and praying that the sanatorium would heal the wound—gradually atone for the loss—fill his life with work and satisfaction so that he would in time forget or at least cease to regret its loss. But, she reminded herself, only if he broke with Sylvia Webster. The girl hated the sanatorium—hated the thought of sharing Bruce with others. She wanted him for herself—her man and hers alone. Ruth shrugged.

"She would ruin him," she said to herself. "Destroy his initiative—sap his strength—weaken his resistance until he became a mere *thing*—a kept man whose sole business in life would be to do her bidding. Oh, Bruce, Bruce, can't you see what she would do to you, dear? You're still young. You're brilliant. You have a great future. Don't yield to her clever trickery, darling. She isn't worth it." She was surprised to find her hands clenched and that her eyes were wet. What a simpleton she was! "I'm acting as if that brother of mine had no sense—no will power," she told herself, and yet no one knew better than she did, the stranglehold a beautiful, unscrupulous woman was capable of wielding, and in the opinion of Ruth Kimberly, Sylvia Webster was just such a woman.

Her eyes focused for a moment on the road in front and she saw a car stop before the nurses' home. It looked like Alan Blake getting out. It was Alan and he ran up the short walk to the porch and rang the bell. She wondered if Jill and he were going some place—and where. She felt a brief pang of disappointment. She had other plans for her favorite nurse.

Yes, there they came, Jill wearing her fur coat and the provocative, perky green hat that was so becoming. They went toward Westhaven. Perhaps they were going to church. Suddenly she had a yearning to leave everything and go, too. But one of them should be at the sanatorium and Bruce had left. She turned restlessly and went into her own office.

Someone brought her a tray and she ate her lunch at her desk. She heard the church-goers return but remained where she was. It was there Bruce found her a few minutes later.

"Busy?" he asked, wandering about the small room. "I looked for you before I left. I wanted to tell you I had received a call from the Center. Wanted me to sit in on a conference. Very interesting. They are planning some drastic changes over there, Ruth." He came to sit on a corner of her desk, his fine eyes smoldering with something, whether resentment or satisfaction, she couldn't tell. "Perhaps one might consider it a compliment, but I figure it was just plain, unadulterated gall. I was invited to give up my job here and become a member of the staff at the Center—sort of resident bigwig—glorified factotum—holding the fort when other and supposedly abler men happened to be busy. Meeting people curious and otherwise—explaining, advising, diagnosing—but only conditionally, mind you—the final word was not to be mine but Newcomb's. Now I ask you, Ruth, do I look like that sort of idiot?"

Ruth's laugh was indignant. "What did you tell them, Bruce? Did you put them in their place once and for all? And whose brilliant idea was it, though I'll wager I can guess." Her eyes snapped with anger.

"Well," Bruce said slowly, "it smells amazingly like Sam Tillotson. He wasn't at the meeting today for some reason. I wonder why. He mentioned something of the sort at Christmas, but I thought I had made myself clear at that time. Why can't people understand that I intend staying here at the sanatorium—making a success of it? Have you any idea, Ruth?"

"Yes, Bruce, I have," Ruth told him. "But you wouldn't like it if I told you, so I will keep still."

Bruce frowned. "You blame Sylvia, don't you?" he said sharply. "Do you think you are being quite fair to her, Ruth?"

"Fair? I think I have always been fair, Bruce—and honest, as well. Sam Tillotson is Sylvia's godfather as well as her uncle. He is president of the Board of Trustees of both the

101

Center and City Hospital and of half a dozen other enterprises in Westhaven. Sylvia has always boasted she could wind him round her finger. Draw your own conclusions, my dear brother. One doesn't have to be particularly astute to reach a logical solution." She shoved back her chair and stood up, tall and slender. She laid a sisterly hand on his arm. "Don't let us quarrel over Sylvia Webster," she went on. "Now to change the subject to one nearer home—Doctor Reynolds was, for a moment only, interested in our experiment—you know, clay modeling. I believe we can gradually work him into it. He made something he called a deer but which might have been anything. At least he seemed to be quite normal for that few seconds. I am encouraged, however, and I wish you could manage to be present during the next lesson."

"I hope you haven't given him tools—but of course you wouldn't. It may work. Occupational therapy so often works seeming miracles in such cases. Poor chap! Do you know, Ruth, he was an exceptionally brilliant man? Overwork."

"Of course," his sister agreed, relieved to be off the controversial subject, "and he will be again. Kimberly Sanatorium is the place for him. I have implicit faith in it." She laughed and he smiled at her enthusiasm. "And it isn't just conceit," she went on more soberly. "We know what we are trying to do and with God's help we shall leave no stone unturned—no effort untried to accomplish it. Had your lunch, Bruce? The church-goers have just returned and I'm sure there is still plenty in the staff dining room. I think I shall go with you. I feel the need of another cup of coffee."

14

THE WEBSTER MANSION was ablaze from attic to basement. It was a great occasion, for the Websters were entertaining nobility. Sylvia's parents had returned from Florida via New York for the affair, as had several friends and intimates of the family. Westhaven advertised the party as "the most important social event of the winter season." Both Ruth and her brother were, of course, invited as was Peter Allison and, oddly enough, Jill Ordway, but not Jeff Thomas. Ruth pleaded a heavy sched-

102

ule and Jill that she was to be on night duty; but the two young men accepted the invitation, although Bruce hesitated because of the puzzling condition of one of the patients at the sanatorium.

"But you won't be away more than four or five hours at the most, Bruce," his sister reminded him. "Rod is no worse that I can see. You said yourself that no doubt he would remain in his present condition for days—maybe weeks. Doctor Judson will be here and Doctor Thomas, too, if we need him. You run along and enjoy yourself. You need the change and relaxation. If anything untoward occurs we'll call you."

"There's something about that boy that bothers me, Ruth," Bruce murmured, almost absently. "There are times when I think he's more aware of his surroundings than he admits. Jill said much the same thing. It would almost seem as if he were waiting his chance to do something—spring a surprise of some sort. He used to have that reputation, you know. I dislike leaving under the circumstances." His eyes clouded, then he shrugged and grinned down at her. "I suppose I am an old granny, Ruth; but these things get hold of a chap and he can't seem to shake them off."

"Well, you'd better shake this off," Ruth told him firmly. "That is one thing we must guard against—letting our job completely possess us. Give my regrets to Sylvia and tell her I should like her to lunch with me one day soon—if she is staying on and cares to."

Bruce's face cleared. "The more I think about it, the more convinced I am that the best solution of our continued misunderstandings would be marriage. After all, Sylvia has waited a long time. Neither of us expected any such delay and no doubt it was all my fault—my unholy pride just wouldn't let me accept anything from her." He sighed. "But after all, what does money matter when two people love each other."

Ruth said nothing for a long moment but her heart sank. She had hoped against hope that Bruce was beginning to see the light—that the break would become permanent—perhaps that Sylvia would meet someone else or that she would become weary of waiting. Now it seemed that it was Bruce who had tired of the delay.

She sighed and said, "Of course you must do as you think best, Bruce, but——"

"Don't say it, Ruth. I know you and Sylvia will probably never become intimate, but for my sake I hope you will try to be friends. I could not endure having you unhappy. After all, we have weathered many storms together and no one—not even my wife, when and if I have one—will separate us. That's a promise, my dear. I mean it."

"*You* may mean it, Bruce," Ruth told him somewhat grimly, "but you don't take Sylvia into account. However, I have said all I shall ever say. I want your happiness more than anything in the world." She drew his face down to hers and kissed him warmly.

"You will surely call me if I am needed. I won't go unless you promise," Bruce said doubtfully.

"Of course," his sister assured him. "But what is likely to happen that we can't handle?"

"I don't know—exactly; but I have a hunch."

"Oh, you and your hunches. Run along, darling. Have a grand time and don't worry about us here."

Bruce met Peter Allison as he left his car in the side yard of the spacious Webster estate and the two walked to the entrance together.

"Ruth didn't come with you, Doc?" Peter asked, disappointment in his voice. "She was invited, I know. And Miss Ordway. What happened? On duty?"

"We couldn't both be away and Ruth decided to be the one to stay. Ordway is on night duty just now and of course couldn't leave."

"I thought she was special day nurse for Doctor Bradley."

"She was until this new case arrived. Rodney Kent—a manic depressive. Another returned veteran—released after two years in a concentration camp. With his reputation I can't understand how they managed to keep him two years. Jill has been so successful with such cases that we borrowed her temporarily from Bradley. In fact, when he heard about it, he insisted she take over the case."

"A pretty swell guy, Doctor Bradley. Some day I'll have to tell you something he did that I'm sure will surprise you. You have no idea of the number of friends and well-wishers you have. It's a great old world, fella, and don't you ever forget it."

And Bruce, who had been trying to shake off the feeling of

104

depression at leaving the sanatorium, laughed lightly. "There are times when I thoroughly agree with you, Pete."

Sylvia was in her element. The rooms were crowded with the elite of Westhaven and points east and south and everyone greeted the two young men enthusiastically. Mrs. Webster smiled coolly as she greeted Bruce but gushed over Pete. Sylvia's father, on the other hand, seemed more than usually jovial, chiding both young men for remaining in Westhaven when Florida provided so many advantages.

Sylvia slipped her arm in Bruce's and murmured for his ear alone, "Darling—I was so afraid you wouldn't come." She pressed his arm, then turned to the guests of honor. "I want you to meet two very special friends of mine—Sir Arthur Banting and Lady Muriel Cokes-Ampry—Doctor Bruce Kimberly. Oh, Pete—so glad you could come. You're such a busy man these days that I scarcely ever see you. I was beginning to wonder if, since joining the sanatorium project, you, too, had become involved as Bruce here has. So sorry your sister and your nurse couldn't make it, Doctor." Her voice was silky and yet Bruce detected that old familiar note of jealousy.

They shook hands with the tall, extremely ugly young Englishman and the florid, horsey-looking middle-aged woman beside him. Bruce decided Sir Arthur might prove interesting but shied away from the woman. He detested horsey women. Sylvia tried to keep the newcomers close to her but some of her friends had other ideas and they were soon in the midst of a rather hilarious crowd.

There was dancing later in the huge ballroom at the top of the house, and games—billiards and bridge or poker—in the game room downstairs. Everything was very gay, if a bit noisy. An elaborate buffet was served before midnight, and even as they sampled the rich food, Bruce and Peter wondered how soon they could break away. Bruce had an uncanny feeling that he should not have come and Pete was plainly beginning to be bored. Sylvia sought them out.

"Don't be uneasy, darling," she rebuked Bruce, and drew him aside. "It's early yet and your old sanatorium will still be there when you get back. Come, let's dance. Do you know you haven't been to see me in weeks?" she reminded him as they circled the room. "Not that I have missed you too much. There has been so much going on—such thrilling things, Bruce—you don't know."

"I think I do know, Sylvia," Bruce said. "But I have been busy. We must have a talk, my dear," he told her hesitantly. Somehow things seemed different right now. "I hope to have a little more leisure after a bit and——"

"You do? When?" the girl cried, a note of triumph discernible. "Fine! I have been waiting for you to see the light." Her hand touched his cheek. "You're thin, Bruce. You have been working too hard. You stick too closely to that place and——"

"I should be leaving, dear," he told her as the music stopped and they found themselves near a door. "I promised to be back——"

Sylvia's face clouded. "Stay for a while after the others leave, darling. They will be going soon. I, too, feel that I must have a talk with you—it has been so long and——"

"Doc, you're wanted at the sanatorium at once," Peter Allison said quickly, ignoring Sylvia and her angry protest. "It seems they have been calling you ever since ten o'clock. I don't understand why you weren't told. Something's gone wrong out there and they need you. I'll go along. 'Night, Syl. Nice party."

Without a word to anyone Bruce Kimberly left the room and ran down the stairs, retrieved his coat and fled, followed closely by Peter Allison.

He didn't hear Sylvia's low, angry cry of, "If you go now, you need never come back."

At least it didn't register—then. He knew he had never before been so angry. This was the end. He could never forgive this.

"Take it easy, Doc," Peter warned as he reached his car.

Bruce didn't answer. The two cars raced through town and out the two-mile country road with ever-increasing speed and swerved into the sanatorium grounds in record time. Bruce leapt from the car and bounded up the steps to the front door. Ruth met him—she was white-faced and heavy-eyed.

"What is it?" he asked through grim lips. "What happened?"

"It was Rod. He went berserk."

"Jill? Did he hurt Jill?"

"Knocked her down—blacked her eye, but otherwise she's

all right. Why didn't you come when I first called you, Bruce? He wasn't dangerous then—merely restless and talkative. Judson tried to give him a hypo but he fought him off. Broke his arm. It was Jeff Thomas who subdued him in the end. Believe me, we have had a hectic time of it here for the past few hours. Did you have a nice time at the party? But of course you must have." Her voice dripped sarcasm, and Peter Allison was surprised at the change in the usually calm, serene Ruth Kimberly. She was plainly angry and thoroughly disgusted with her brother.

"Wait a minute, Ruth," Peter said before Bruce could explain. In fact he was already sprinting up the stairs. "Your message was never delivered. Probably Sylvia gave orders that Doc was not to be called to the phone or given any messages. It would be just like her, you know. Spoiled brat! Don't blame Doc, Ruth. He's all broken up over it and I have a notion this finishes him with the beauteous Sylvia Webster for all time."

Ruth's mouth trembled. She wanted to cry—a superintendent of nurses—twenty-nine years old—wanting to bawl like a ten-year-old. And Peter seemed to sense her emotion, for he took her in his arms and whispered, "Go on, darling. Cry your heart out. It will do you good and my shoulder is quite comfortable. There—there!" he crooned, patting her back in what he no doubt considered the approved method. "Everything is going to be all right." After a few minutes he thrust a square of immaculate linen into her clenched hand and urged tenderly, "Blow your nose, honey, and wipe your eyes and smile for Pete. That's the girl!"

"I'm—I'm—so—ashamed, P-Pete!" she gulped.

"No need to be. You know I'm your business manager—until I am promoted to something better. I'm here to act as buffer when needed and can produce a broad shoulder for weeping—your weeping, of course. I'm sort of exclusive, darling. I'll have no other gal's tears dampening my shoulder except yours. Is it a deal?"

Ruth was too bewildered to answer. He patted her shoulder and went on, "Lay off Doc, Ruth. He's really shot to pieces."

"And do you think—— No, it would be too good to be true."

"I know what you mean, Ruth," Pete said, "and I think it's true all right. Wait and see. Now I think you had better go to bed, young lady. You look all in. I'll stick around until Doc comes back and maybe we can find some good strong coffee. I feel in need of a stimulant."

"I'll make it right now," Ruth said, suddenly her calm, efficient self, turning toward the kitchen. Pete followed. And when Bruce came downstairs a few minutes later, he joined them there. His sister and Pete were preparing toast, scrambled eggs and coffee. The talk after that was quiet and sane. Ruth gave a detailed account of what happened in Rodney Kent's room earlier in the evening and Bruce listened silently, his face grave and concerned. They were still talking when Jeff Thomas joined them. A strip of adhesive tape adorned his chin and a lump the size of a walnut decorated his right temple. He grinned at the others.

"You ought to see the other fellow," he told them.

"I have," Bruce said, "and he is sleeping as quietly as an infant and without a scratch. How did you do it, Jeff?"

"Judo. Came in handy. Kent's a tough baby but I don't think we'll have any more trouble with him. Honestly, I think the explosion did him good—released something—got rid of poison that had been accumulating inside his cranium for months —maybe years. As you say, Doc, he's sleeping the sleep of innocence. Already he looks different. Probably won't recall anything of what happened tonight. Poor Jill! A more surprised gal you never saw in your life. People just don't punch our Jill, Doc. It just isn't done. Wait till you see the shiner. It's a humdinger."

Bruce scowled. "We can't have things like this occurring here. Perhaps we should have a male nurse—one for such cases. Are you sure it was nothing worse than a black eye, Jeff —no concussion?"

"Well, she went off home under her own power, Doc, so I guess she wasn't too badly hurt. I doctored the eye and gave her a sedative, and except for a splitting headache in the morning or for a couple of days, maybe, I imagine she will be all right. Judson didn't come off so easily. Arm snapped clean. Between us, Ruth and I reduced the fracture and he, too, is off to bed. I'm the sole survivor—that is, unless you decide to take over, Doc. Though after your heavy date I guess you need a little shut-eye. I don't mind. Run along—all of you. It's time for my rounds. 'Night. See you in the morning."

108

"I don't feel right about Jill, Ruth," Bruce said to his sister as they entered their own home a few minutes later. "Are you sure she was all right when she left? Do you suppose I should take a look at her now?"

"Oh, I don't think so, Bruce. Jeff gave her a sedative and without doubt she is asleep. Wait until morning. We'll both go see her. She was really wonderful, Bruce. Didn't show the least fear—that is, when she regained consciousness. She was out for only a minute but she got up and tried to help Judson, who was helpless in Rod's hands. Fortunately, Jeff had been having a few stolen minutes—quite against the rules, of course —with Ann Burke. She happened to be on call upstairs and he heard the commotion and raced to the rescue. It was all over in a minute then, and Rod was back in bed sort of dazed but completely subdued. No, I don't think there is any need to worry about Jill. She'll be all right—off duty for a few days —but perfectly well otherwise."

"That I will have to see," Bruce said to himself as he followed his sister upstairs for what remained of the night.

## 15

IT WAS FORTUNATE that nothing of the story of Rodney Kent's outbreak penetrated to the other patients at Kimberly and it was as Jeff said—the explosion seemed to have worked a miracle in the young man's condition. When Bruce called on him the next morning he greeted him pleasantly—spoke of the dreariness of the weather and wanted to get up. He flexed his arms in demonstration of his well-being and grinned like a small boy. No one mentioned his treatment of Jill and if he recalled anything he failed to speak of it. But from time to time Bruce detected a puzzled look in the patient's eyes as if he couldn't quite comprehend—explain conditions and surroundings to himself.

Jimmy Anthony, an interne at City Hospital, came out to take Doctor Judson's place and the sanatorium settled down to its usual calm. Bruce and his sister made their call at the nurses' home and saw Jill who grinned wryly at them and held her head, moving restlessly from side to side on her pillow.

"I certainly have a beautiful hangover this morning," she told them whimsically. "How is our patient and—oh, yes, Doctor Judson?"

"Rod looks and acts innocent as a baby. He appears to be quite normal this morning and apparently has forgotten all about his spree," Bruce told her, his fingers on her pulse. "Doctor Judson is resting quietly and his wife is having a grand time fussing over him. This is going to be a pleasant respite for him. Lucky for him it was his left arm. We have borrowed one of City's internes—Jim Anthony. Pretty good, from all accounts. Well, take it easy, my girl, and don't worry about a thing. I'll be in again."

He went out and Ruth remained for a moment longer. "Don't you dare show your face at the sanatorium until you have quite recovered, Jill. The rest will do you good. Sleep and rest—everything is going to be all right—everything." She left the room and Jill was puzzled to know just what she meant.

Alan Blake called repeatedly and couldn't understand why Jill refused to see him. At last he insisted on coming in and Mrs. Davis suggested he sit down in the living room and she would see if Jill would see him. The girl's eye had paled considerably and she felt that it would not be apt to cause comment even if Alan happened to notice it. She followed the housemother down to the living room. Alan's greeting was a mixture of delight and sympathy.

"Feeling better?" he asked, her hand in both of his. "I've been terribly worried about you. No one seemed to know just what ailed you and I began to wonder if it was I—if you had decided to cross me off your list of friends. I'm vastly relieved, Jill."

"Oh, I'm all right now," Jill told him. "It was just one of those things you know that happens sometimes," she went on, deciding it best to explain a bit. After all, a black eye was nothing out of the ordinary these days and anyway, he would know it sooner or later. "You see, Alan, I happened to connect too forcibly with a blunt object and in consequence suffered a terrific headache and a black eye and you know no nurse can appear before her patient wearing signs of conflict even though she has a perfectly legitimate excuse. It just isn't

110

done." She laughed lightly and Alan turned her around and gave a long, low whistle.

"Gosh!" he exclaimed after a minute. "That must have been some shiner. And I never supposed nursing was to be classed among hazardous occupations. Do you dare come out for a ride, Jill? It's not too bad a day—not cold at least. You could wear dark glasses if you like. We could have dinner someplace and maybe dance. It's what you need. You look peaked. Too much work and no play. I'll do some prescribing for you."

"I think not, Blake," Doctor Kimberly said from the hall which he had just entered. "We can't risk a cold in that eye. How are you feeling today, Ordway?" he wanted to know. His voice was coldly professional and somehow Jill resented it.

"How can she take cold in a heated car?" Alan demanded.

"My eye is about well, Doctor," Jill told him, wilfully deciding she wanted to go with Alan. "I haven't been out in three days and I need fresh air. I expect to be back on duty tomorrow night—maybe even tonight."

The doctor shook his head. "Of course you must do as you think best," he said stiffly. "But as your doctor I would suggest a couple of days' complete rest and quiet. I am sorry to have interrupted. Forgive me." He turned and the front door slammed behind him.

"Crusty cuss, isn't he?" Alan said. "But inasmuch as you aren't a child and he doesn't own you, I suggest we start."

"Perhaps he's right, Alan," Jill demurred. "After all, he is a doctor and my employer. Why not stay here and visit for a while? I could even make chocolate or coffee and we could have a sort of lunch right here. I don't know about dinner. We don't usually have a man to dinner, though perhaps Mrs. Davis could even provide for that."

Alan shook his head stubbornly. "Are you afraid of Kimberly, Jill?" he asked.

"Of course not," the girl replied. "Why do you say that? But he is my boss——"

"What if he is? Oh, come on—it's only a little after five. We might even take in a movie—part of it anyway. Be your age. Of course, we could go over to the farm and have dinner there. I want you to meet my people anyway—Mother and Dad have wanted you to come out and Mom intends sending

111

you a written invitation—if that's what you are waiting for. I've talked about you to them and they're interested in you and in the sanatorium as well."

"But I don't want to meet anyone until my eye is quite normal again, Alan," Jill protested. "Oh, all right, but let's go somewhere quiet. There's a place on Grand Street in Westhaven that isn't too bad. Maybe you know it. I went there with Jeff Thomas once. The food was excellent and we danced afterward. I think I shall like doing that, Alan. Wait until I change into something different. I won't be long. Amuse yourself with these magazines," she said pointing to the pile on the table nearby.

"Honestly, your eye isn't at all bad," he assured her. "It seems worse to you than it actually is. You don't need dark glasses. Don't be long, Jill."

Feeling somewhat guilty, Jill joined Alan Blake and hoped Kim wouldn't know that she had deliberately ignored his advice. She was surprised and delighted to find that no one appeared to notice her eye. They sat through the last part of a movie, then went to the Grand Street place. They found the dinner all that she had promised and they danced until well after ten when Jill insisted they leave.

"It has been swell, Alan," she told him as they sped along the snowy road toward the sanatorium and the nurses' home. "I was getting bored with my own society and needed something of the sort. You're a pretty good diagnostician, and I liked your prescription. I feel so very much better. Thanks a lot."

"How about coming out home tomorrow, Jill? Sis and the infant will be there then and you can meet the entire family. I want you to like them. I know they will like you—can't help it. Will you come?"

"But—but, Alan, I don't want to meet people until my eye is entirely well."

"Don't be silly. You're too sensitive. No one paid any attention to it tonight, did they? Well, they won't tomorrow either and it will be even less noticeable then. I'll be along soon after two tomorrow and we'll have a nice long day. I'll show you the farm—our prize pigs and cattle and my own special mare. She's a honey—almost human. Do you ride, Jill?"

"I used to, but haven't had a chance lately."

"We'll soon remedy that," Alan said with enthusiasm. "Sis keeps her saddle horse out at the farm and you can use him. We can have some dandy rides up into the hills. Spring isn't too far off and I'll really show you the country around here. There's nothing better anywhere. Sleep well, dar-ling," he whispered and drew her close for a moment. Jill thought he was going to kiss her and supposed she would have to submit, but he pressed his cold cheek against hers and let her go. She got out before Alan could get around to open the door and ran up the snowy walk to the front porch, while the young man followed more slowly. The door was unlocked and she turned to wave. Alan stood, his foot on the lower step.

"Good night, Alan," she said softly. "Thank you for— everything."

"See you tomorrow—at two," he said and remained to watch her open the door and disappear inside. Then he turned and went back to his car. Why hadn't he kissed her? He had the chance and maybe she wouldn't have repulsed him. But he wasn't sure and with a girl like Jill Ordway one had to go slowly.

"A registered package for you, Doc," Peter Allison said as he stopped at Bruce Kimberly's office before going on to his own farther down the hall. He had been enjoying his job of business manager for the Kimberly Sanatorium now for some time and everything seemed to run smoothly. It was thought at first he should have a desk in the Chief's office but Pete felt he could work better by himself, so a tiny room was found for him and he crowded into it a desk, an ever increasing number of files, a chair or two, a typewriter and a telephone. And there he spent several hours each day in complete absorption.

"Someone sending you valuables, fella?" he asked incuriously. "I signed for it, although old Bonner looked sort of suspicious. What you need is a secretary, old man. Ever think of that? Gosh! What a mess! Don't you ever clear it up?"

"Oh, Ruth does it in her spare time. She's an excellent typist, you know, and in a couple of hours after she takes hold there won't be a loose end anywhere." Bruce slit another envelope and grinned at his friend. "And listen, lug—we're not

**113**

making money as fast as you would like me to think. Secretaries cost plenty these days, or didn't you know that?"

He examined the registered package for a moment, then frowned, a slow color creeping to his hairline. He dropped the unopened package into a drawer and slammed it shut. Peter Allison turned toward the door then took a folded newspaper from his pocket and tossed it on his Chief's desk.

"Interesting news in the morning paper, Doc. Might do you good to read it. Be seeing you." He closed the door softly behind him and went on to his own office. His mail was heavy this morning and he spent a busy two hours answering letters of inquiry, planning a new advertising campaign, ordering necessary supplies from the list Ruth had left on his desk and paying the most urgent of the bills. At last he sat back, whistling softly as he covered his machine. He was happier than he had been in years. He was doing just what he had long dreamed of doing. The sanatorium had been something of an obsession with him ever since Doctor Morgan took over his father's stock—the stock that should one day have been his. He was determined to make something outstanding of this place. He had known and admired Bruce Kimberly for many years. He knew a few of the patients—one or two intimately. Mrs. Botany was an old friend of his family and he considered Doctor Bradley one of the world's best. He answered "Come" at the light knock on his closed door. Ruth Kimberly poked her head inside.

"I'm in a rush, Pete," she told him. "Did you know Sylvia had left Westhaven? That she had gone to Florida? You did? Why didn't you tell me? What does it mean? Does Bruce know?"

"He should by this time," Pete said, snapping a rubber band about the outgoing mail. "I gave him a copy of the morning paper. It's all there—the private plane—the titled guests and the beauteous Sylvia with her long-suffering parents flying down for what remains of the winter. It seems they left day before yesterday. I didn't know that."

"I wonder—" she began and stopped.

"Don't," Pete told her. "Everything will work out fine—if you don't rush things. The guy's probably feeling sunk right now. I was, myself—back in my callow youth—when she turned me down. But one recovers from such things—espe-

114

cially if the wound isn't very deep. What's your particular rush? Come on in and sit."

Ruth came into the room. "I heard that you were an old beau of hers, Pete," she said dryly. "Maybe——"

"Nothing doing," the young man interrupted. "She's no longer my type. By the way, how's the black eye coming along —and Judson's arm? That certainly was some excitement you had here."

"You don't know the half of it," Ruth said. "Jill Ordway is just about ready to return to duty and Doctor Judson's arm seems to be doing nicely. I don't think he is worrying unduly. I know he expects to take on a few light duties next week. But do you know, it's the strangest thing to watch Rodney Kent. He appears to be completely unaware of his outrageous behavior, though he wears a puzzled frown whenever he looks at Betty Lundy, his substitute night nurse. But he asks no questions and no explanations are vouchsafed. He's quiet as a lamb and begs to get up. We shall let him tomorrow, I think, if all goes well."

"His time's nearly up, anyway, isn't it?" Pete asked. "There's a letter here—somewhere—I had it a minute ago—mean to pass it over to the Chief. It's his department, not mine. Gosh! Where did I put the darned thing? Oh, of course, I filed it. Methodical Pete—that's me." He rose and opened a filing case. "Here it is. His father is ready to take him on to Minnesota. Think he will be able to travel by plane, Ruth?" He replaced the filing case and sat down again.

"I suppose so. Physically the man is perfectly well and now that his mental condition seems to have improved I should say he is quite ready to leave. But I don't think his father will take him to Minnesota now, Pete. I predict he will take him home. After all, his stay at Kimberly has produced the results desired —and that we expected. Yes, we did, Pete. I have great faith in Kimberly. I want to try an experiment though. I have been wondering what reaction, if any, he will have when he sees Jill Ordway again. He watches the door so expectantly and he looks puzzled and almost dazed every time he looks at Lundy that he must have some recollection of his former nurse. Bruce isn't in favor of Jill's going back to him at all, but Jeff Thomas and I are frankly curious."

"How about Jeff? Did he remember him at all?"

Ruth shook her head. "Apparently not." She stood up. "I've got to run, Pete. Want me to give Bruce that letter?"

"If you like. I've got to go over to the bank. Any errands I can do for you or your charges?"

"I think not, thanks," the superintendent of nurses said as she left the room. "I shall have to go into town in a day or two and everything can wait until then."

The door closed and Peter Allison slipped into his overc' and galoshes, tucked his hat under his arm and slammed ⌐ front door after him. He immediately snapped his fingers.

"That's something I have to do," he said to the world at large. "There's got to be a silencer put on that door, or else," he grinned to himself, "Pete Allison will have to learn not to slam it."

## 16

RUTH KIMBERLY WENT into her brother's office almost timidly. How had Bruce taken the break with Sylvia Webster—her run-out? He sat with his back to the door, a jeweler's box in his hands. He made as if to thrust it back into the drawer but Ruth had already seen it. She ran to him, her face sympathetic, her hands tender upon his shoulders.

"Darling," she said softly, "don't take it too hard. She isn't worth it."

"You never liked her, did you?" he said almost roughly. "I have always known it. And somehow, in my own heart, I have always felt she was not for me. Since becoming crippled I have been increasingly aware of it."

"Crippled!" Ruth cried indignantly. "*You're* not crippled. How can you say such a thing?" His sister thought she detected a trace of a Sylvia jibe in that remark. "Why, you are approaching the very height of your career, Bruce Kimberly. Don't let me hear any more of such morbid drivel. It isn't like you. Snap out of it!" She spread before him the letter Pete had given her. "How about this, Bruce? Shall we permit Rod to leave as scheduled? He seems to be all right but it is for you to say—of course."

Doctor Kimberly focused his eyes on the closely typed page

116

before him and for a moment saw nothing, then with an effort he straightened and read rapidly. "Of course, that was the arrangement at the time, but now that the fellow is practically well, his father may have other plans. I shall wire him to come at once. He may wish him to stay on for a few days longer or may want to take him directly home. What do you advise, Ruth?"

"I hope his father removes him at once," Ruth said grimly. "Anyway, we can use his room."

Bruce patted his sister's hand. "Poor Ruthy!" he murmured.

Ruth withdrew her hand. Her lips were a straight line. "I think I shall be a long time forgiving Sylvia Webster for neglecting to give you my message, Bruce," she said shortly. "As it happened, it was merely serious—it might have been tragic."

"I know. I know," her brother agreed, "and I think it was that very act of selfish thoughtlessness that tore the veil from my eyes, Ruth." He threw back his shoulders and lifted his head. "I suppose I should be grateful that things have ended as they have. We should never have been happy. Sylvia was not meant to be a doctor's wife and I suppose I am too opinionated—or too pig-headed—to ever become a satisfactory husband. My work will always come first and no woman will stand for that—or will she?"

"The right woman will, my dear," Ruth told him, patting his shoulder affectionately. "And by the way, have you noticed an attractive young man who seems to be courting our Jill Ordway? The extremely eligible Alan Blake. The Blakes have a big estate—though they call it a farm—just west of here. Acres and acres, and Alan is the only son. I understand they have a daughter—married and living in Meredith. From all reports Jill would be doing well if she married young Blake, but I am selfish enough to want to keep her here. Jill's something pretty special. I love that girl, Bruce."

"How long has this been going on, Ruth?" Bruce demanded truculently. "I came upon them a day or so ago planning a visit to Westhaven for dinner and dancing. The day was blustery and with that bad eye and her condition of shock I frankly disapproved of the venture; but they disregarded my advice I understand and carried out their plans. I supposed Jill had a level head—was too sensible to fall for a country Lothario no matter how much money he had. But I guess girls are all alike.

117

When is she returning to duty? It seems to me she is taking her time about it."

"Less than a week, my dear. She is starting tomorrow night."

"Not going back on the Kent case, Ruth. Doctor Bradley has been very generous in allowing her to be transferred, but after that *contretemps* it is only fair to them both that she return to him."

"Am I superintendent of nurses, my dear brother, or am I not?" Ruth chided. "I must do as I think best. I think Jill should go back to Kent for no other reason than to see just how much of that affair he recalls. I'm sure the girl wants to go back. She feels somehow that she failed him and the going back will have a salutary effect. Someone will be near just in case there is trouble but I am sure there won't be."

"All right," Bruce said grimly. "If you insist on this—this strange idea *I* shall make it a point to be present."

"As you wish," Ruth said, a little wave of laughter welling up inside her. "I intended being not too far away, myself. We can't risk having anything happening to our Jill, can we, dear?"

Bruce stared at her blandly innocent eyes for a long moment then turned away, his face red with annoyance. Ruth hurried from the room and mounted the stairs with a feeling almost of relief. She imagined her adored brother wasn't too deeply hurt. She felt that now, perhaps, he had some chance of happiness. She knew that with Sylvia Webster any possibility of it was practically nil.

"Well, what do you know about this, Jill?" Ann Burke asked. The two girls had been doing a bit of laundering late that same evening. After rolling her precious nylons in a bath towel, Ann had picked up the morning paper from the stand where someone had left it earlier. "Look here, Juliet. Sylvia —the Chief's glamor gal, has left Westhaven—gone south with—Listen. 'Accompanying the Websters in their private plane were their distinguished guests, Sir Arthur Banting and Lady Muriel Cokes-Ampry.' What's distinguished about them, Jill? Never heard of 'em. Did you? Maybe that's what's been eating our Chief lately—maybe this Banting guy has cut him out with Sylvia. Three cheers to that! What do you know? Well, Doc Kimberly is darned lucky if he only knew it. Jeff

118

will probably weep for joy. The fair Sylvia's poison to him. What did you say?"

"Nothing," Jill murmured, her face hidden as she rummaged through a closet for something—she didn't know what.

"Oh, who cares anyway?" Ann went on, tossing the paper aside. "What I want to know is what's cooking between you and the Blake hopeful? Seems to me the lug's attentions are getting serious. When a guy trots a gal off for his family's inspection it means—tra-la-la-la—Ump-ti-t-dee and the long aisle with orchids and what have you. I doubt if you could do better, Juliet. Jeff says the Blakes have scads of money and Alan's the only son. It will all be his some day. How did you like his people—snooty, were they? So many rich folks are—like the Websters."

Jill came out of the closet. "They were sweet, Ann. I liked them a lot. I was surprised they seemed so friendly—almost as if they had known me always. They have a huge place. I imagine it is delightful in summer. I was surprised at their interest in the sanatorium, too. They look upon it as a sort of landmark —an institution of which they are proud. I had to tell them all about it—the changes being planned and of the help it had been to the returned veterans who had been treated here. They were particularly interested in the Kimberlys. It seems the doctor had built up something of a reputation as a surgeon. They haven't met him but expect to very soon, as they planned a visit here. Alan laughed and told them Kim was a 'sourpuss' and warned his mother to watch her step."

"Why did he say that, Jill? I didn't even know they had met."

Jill bit her lip. "Oh, one afternoon—when I was still nursing my black eye—Alan came and insisted I go into town for dinner and dancing. He had his car, but I held back, disliking to show myself in public. However, Alan was pretty persistent and just then Doctor Kimberly walked in. Probably wondered why I wasn't back at work. Anyway, he objected to my going out and Alan wasn't very polite to him."

"But you went, didn't you? Of course you did. After all, the old sanatorium doesn't own us body and soul—though sometimes I have a feeling it thinks it does. Good for you, Juliet! I'm glad to see you showed some spirit. More power to you!"

119

"Oh, it wasn't that exactly," Jill protested. "I was just fed up with staying in. And stop calling me Juliet."

"Sure—sure," Ann agreed. "Coming back with us tomorrow? Seems to me I heard something of the sort. Where you going? Back with Kent, or has the lend-lease expired? You certainly had a cinch with Doctor Bradley. I wish I had your drag, my girl. How do you do it?"

"I'm going back to Kent—for a while. He's leaving very soon. I sort of feel I fell down there———"

"I'll say you did," laughed Ann. "Jeff told me you were out cold for a minute or two."

"Oh, I don't mean that. I mean I failed some way and I have to return to sort of regain my self-respect, if you know what I mean."

"I know. But suppose he feels like a return bout—blacks your other eye, darling? What then?"

"He won't," Jill said firmly. "I was taken completely by surprise that time. I'll be ready for him if he attempts anything of the sort again—which, of course, he won't. That brainstorm did something for him—cleared the air—removed some pressure—or something. I have an idea he will recover completely very soon now—if he hasn't already. Jeff was marvelous, Ann. He held that big, husky fellow and with his two hands took every bit of fight out of him, then tossed him on the bed as if he were an infant. You never saw a more surprised person in your life. The vagueness that has persisted since he was brought here vanished as if by magic and he turned on his side and promptly went to sleep. Evidently that particular therapy was effective in his case."

"Just the same, I think we should have a couple of strong-arm men in our midst, Jill. Some of these ex-G. I.'s are pretty rugged individuals. I heard the Chief and Jeff discussing it soon after the affair. Jeff didn't think much of the idea. Says a thing like that wouldn't happen once in a hundred years. After all, Kimberly Sanatorium doesn't go in for that sort of patient, but just the same, it might be a good idea. Don't you think so?"

Jill shook her head. "Oh, I agree with Jeff, Ann. Why, while I was in training I nursed insane patients, delirious patients—even some suffering from D. T.'s—and never had one lay so much as a finger on me. I honestly can't understand what

120

happened this time. It was all so quick—so sudden." She laughed ruefully. "I'm just a bit ashamed of myself, Ann," she went on. "I should have been on the alert. After all, we are trained to expect emergencies. No, my dear, I'm not at all pleased with my part in the fracas, and shall feel better after I have been back there."

"You're welcome," the other girl said, gathering up her laundry. "If it were I, I think I should demand relief and compensation. After all, we aren't supposed to submit to such indignities."

"Oh, forget it, Ann. I'm none the worse for it, in fact, I have had a good rest, plus several excellent dinners, a few dances and time for reading and meditation. There, I'm finished, and if you will get off my bed and take yourself down the hall to your own room, I think I'll try to get some sleep. Believe it or not, my friend, social life can be very tiring—especially when one isn't used to it. 'Night, darling. See you in the morning."

The door closed behind Ann Burke and Jill picked up the newspaper and sat down to read the account of the Webster flitting. Just what did it mean—if anything? And what difference could it possibly make to her, anyway? She tossed the paper aside and slowly undressed. The night was very dark with neither moon nor star. The wind sighed and moaned through the pines and the girl shivered as she slipped the winter screen in place. Her glance swept the darkness. There was a light in the Kimberly house. The living room, probably. It flickered and she thought it might be firelight. Was Kim brooding there in the dark over his broken romance? Or was it broken? She recalled Ruth saying that everything would be all right. Did she mean anything in particular? But why should she say it to her? Surely she hadn't worn her heart on her sleeve. No. It was just conversation. Ruth had meant nothing specific. She must stop being notional—sensitive. A light came on in the room across the wide expanse of snow that separated the nurses' home from the Chief's house. There, it went out —even the flickering firelight faded. A window bloomed on the next floor to be blacked out as a shade was drawn. Jill sighed and slipped into bed.

"Please God, let me be strong and of good courage," she

121

prayed as she had from the time she entered training. "Help me to be ever useful—give me the grace to say and do the right thing at the right time and keep me from the sin of selfishness——"

17

AT SEVEN O'CLOCK the next day, Jill relieved Mary Blanchard, Rodney Kent's day nurse. Doctor Kimberly was in the room and Ruth was just outside in the corridor with Doctor Thomas who was explaining some new idea he had been working on. If Jill was surprised to see Bruce there she gave no sign but picked up the patient's chart and studied it closely for a moment.

There was a gasp from the bed and the patient exclaimed triumphantly, "Then it wasn't just a dream—I didn't make you up—you're real, aren't you?" Jill swung around. She smiled into the boyish face just now flushed with excitement.

"Of course I'm real," she said.

"Then why did you ditch me?"

"Oh, even a nurse has to have an occasional day off, you know," she smiled.

"A day! You were gone a millennium and I suffered. I had the most awful nightmares. Don't ever do it again, Juliet. I can't stand it."

"Juliet." How was it he knew her name? Until the night of the explosion he was supposed to be in a comatose condition —quite unaware of his surroundings. And then no one called her "Juliet." She had been "Jill" so long that she had almost forgotten it was her name. Was it possible that he had heard Ann Burke, who sometimes liked to tease her—knowing how she disliked her romantic name? She wondered.

"When I leave here," the patient went on happily, "I'm going to take you with me. Did you know that? I can't live without you."

"Nonsense!" Doctor Kimberly said sharply, watching the patient closely. "It isn't at all likely we shall allow you to walk off with one of our best nurses, Kent. We need her here and intend keeping her. Anyway, your father is coming to see

122

you tomorrow and inasmuch as your condition has improved so satisfactorily, will probably want to take you home with him."

"That's what you think," the young man muttered. "I don't intend losing my girl just when I have found her again. If I leave—she leaves with me. That's a promise."

Jill laughed and patted the hand outside the coverlet. "That's what they all say—when convalescing, my friend. It's an excellent sign—shows you are rapidly recovering—running true to form. Think nothing of it, Rodney; after you have been away from the sanatorium for a week or two you'll forget all about it. You're so much better than when I saw you last. I'm very glad." Her warning glance encountered Bruce's questioning gaze and she shook her head. He drew her aside.

"Nervous?" he asked.

"Not a bit," she replied not quite truthfully, but it was not the job or the patient that made her nervous—it was his own presence there. She wished he would go away.

"I'm leaving a sedative," the doctor went on. "See that he takes it not later than nine o'clock. If, by any chance, he becomes excited or unmanageable, ring my office. Yes?" He turned as Ruth entered.

"Oh, I just wanted to see how Rodney is feeling this evening," she said pleasantly—almost maternally. "You're looking fine—and rested. I am glad. I imagine you are anxious to get away from us, aren't you? Well, it won't be long now. We shall miss you, of course. We so often become attached to our guests, you know, although we watch them leave with a feeling of thankfulness that ours has been the privilege of aiding them in regaining their health. I think Mrs. Botany wants to talk with you, Doctor. Mr. Allison is with her."

With a keen side glance at the young patient, Bruce left the room and Ruth sat down beside the bed. "Your father is a very happy man," she told him. "He has been terribly worried about you—calling every day—sometimes twice a day, for a report on your condition. Imagine our joy in being able to announce a complete recovery."

"Why, was I sick?" Rodney asked doubtfully. "I know I had a terrible headache and the most awful nightmares; but I don't think I was really sick. If I was, it was due to the loss of Juliet. Now that she is back I'm okay. She smiled and the terror vanished—she waved a magic wand and every ache and pain departed. Do you wonder that I don't want to lose her—ever? Dad will make it worth your while, Miss Kimberly."

"How do you mean?" Ruth laughed. "With money? No, my friend, there isn't enough in the whole world to buy one of our nurses. Why, think of all the others who need their tender care. You're a big boy now and must realize one can't always have the thing one wants—or fancies he wants. Now I've brought you a new puzzle that has stumped mightier brains than yours, Mr. Rodney Kent. Doctor Judson hasn't been able to solve it and neither has your day nurse—yet. I haven't tried but feel sure I could—if I had the time." She laughed and turned the puzzle over to him. "Your father told me you're a whiz at solving puzzles, Rodney, but I have a strong suspicion that this one is quite beyond you. Don't let it keep you awake. Lights out at nine—sharp. Good night—sleep well."

She left the room and Jill followed her into the corridor. "Don't worry about me, Ruth," she told her impulsively. "I'm not in the least nervous. He will be all right—I'm quite sure." And it seemed as if she was correct in her prediction, for when she returned to her patient he was already absorbed in the puzzle the superintendent had brought him. She administered the sedative at nine, made the usual entries on his chart and watched while his eyelids drooped and the puzzle slipped from his nerveless hands.

So much for all the fuss and bother. She felt rather than saw that from time to time during the long quiet night, she and her patient were under surveillance and she felt annoyed. At one o'clock the door-handle turned softly and Ellen Reade beckoned her outside.

"How's the gorilla, Ordway? Your lunch is out here. Gosh, he looks about as dangerous as a kitten!" she grinned as Jill closed the door. "Good-looking, isn't he? Rich, too, they tell me. But with the reputation he's supposed to have you're welcome to him. Hope you like your food, darling. I fixed it myself—your tray, I mean. Had a yen to view the gent."

"Don't talk rubbish, Reade," Jill told her mildly. "The boy was sick—shock and I don't know what all. Those concentration camps weren't especially conducive to steady nerves and iron self-control. Those fellows suffered, and I don't suppose we know the half of it or ever shall. But he's all right now and

124

will be going home tomorrow or next day. Thanks—everything looks grand and am I famished."

"I thought Walker was on call up here tonight, Ordway. But that one is never where she's expected to be. Oh, here she comes—smarty! So she got her own tray. Well, I bet it's no better than yours. Gosh, I'm dead on my feet. I shall certainly be glad when we get more help. This doing double duty isn't all it's cracked up to be. Oh, we all want to see our beloved sanatorium reach prosperity's corner, but we also want to be alive when that elusive corner is reached. I might as well wait until you've finished, Ordway. If I got back downstairs someone will poke another job off on me and I sure need a breather right now." She sank down in the nearest chair, then sprang to her feet as Doctor Kimberly turned a corner of the corridor. Jill, too, arose. He waved them to resume their seats and continued down the long hall, not even stopping at Rodney Kent's door.

Jill went on with her lunch and Ellen whispered wryly, "Guess I'd better vanish before his nibs comes back. I'm out of bounds, just in case you don't know it. S'long. See you some more." She hurried away and Jill finished her lunch quickly. Doctor Anthony was taking Doctor Judson's place until his arm should heal, so just what emergency had brought Doctor Kimberly up here at this hour? She joined Sally Walker for a moment's chat and piled the empty dishes and tray on the dumb-waiter. Doctor Kimberly had not returned.

She went back to her patient. He was sleeping soundly and she sat down at the table with its shaded lamp and picked up the book she had intended reading to Rodney if he should prove restless or wakeful. Again and again she was aware of faint footsteps—a moment's pausing, then slowly growing fainter. For two pins she would go out there and send whoever it was about his business. She didn't like it at all. What sort of a nurse did they think she was to require a bodyguard? Once she opened the door and peered into the dim corridor only to hear the faint sound of stealthy footsteps somewhere beyond her line of vision. She sighed in exasperation and had a fleeting wish that something would happen so she could prove her ability. But nothing did happen and when the first signs of a new day reached her, she raised the shade and looked out upon a bleak, cold March morning. Quarter past six—nearly time

125

for her relief—nearly time for breakfast and she was healthily hungry.

Doctor Kimberly met her as she was going down to breakfast. "Well, how did things go?" he wanted to know—as if he didn't already, Jill asked herself.

"All right," the girl answered somewhat shortly. "He was still sleeping when I left. I didn't expect anything else."

"Any more talk of taking you with him?"

Jill shook her head emphatically. "All that was pure nonsense, of course," she said coolly. "It's just a phase—with convalescing males—even G. I.'s. Nurses are used to it—it doesn't mean a thing. I'm not in the least worried, Doctor—in spite of his reputation for always getting what he wants. And I feel sure he doesn't remember a thing of what happened that night."

"I'm not so sure," the doctor said as he walked away. "And it might be wise of you to avoid being alone—for a few days at least." This last bit of advice was given over his shoulder.

Jill stared at the retreating back. She was angry. What did he think she was—an adolescent—a tender plant, afraid of her shadow, and after all those months abroad! She mixed metaphors indiscriminately while watching the doctor stride back to his office. What was the matter with him? Had he forgotten? She sighed dolefully—all her anger gone and in its place a dull persistent ache that had been with her ever since her arrival in Westhaven. She went slowly in to breakfast.

The meal was good and Jill did full justice to it in spite of her heartache. Ann Burke joined her as she prepared to leave the building.

"I see you're still alive and kicking, darling," Ann said as she linked an arm in that of her friend. "Such solicitude—such care—such—— Gosh, Jill, if I didn't know better I'd say the Chief was getting soft over you. I bet you could cut the glamorous Sylvia out this minute if you put your mind to it. Ever give it a thought, Juliet?"

"Spare me, Ann. I'm sore. They make me sick. All night long I could hear footsteps going back and forth outside the door—made me think of the gestapo. If they could have been where I have been and experienced something of what I have in my short life, I feel sure they would sing a different tune."

"I know," Ann soothed. "Just a pistol-packing mama—or

126

something. Well, one would never think it to look at you. You're the exemplification of pulchritude—the epitome of what every man dreams his wife will be—the gentle, sweet, docile maiden that calls out the chivalry—if any—in every male. You're a fake, Juliet—a menace—a lovely fraud; but I'm crazy about you, just the same. Want to make something of it?"

Jill laughed as the other had intended she should. "I suppose I'm silly to mind it, Ann, but I detest surveillance in any form. I suppose it's the gypsy in me."

"If you're a gypsy I'm a Hottentot," Ann jeered as they parted.

The senior Kent arrived at the sanatorium early that same afternoon and went directly to his son's room. Rodney was being quite unnecessarily fractious and his father grinned happily. For the first time in months his only child was acting natural and he loved it. He rushed into the room, ignoring Bruce's restraining hand, and threw his arms about his son.

"Rodney, my boy! How wonderful to see you so well! I have come to take you home. We brought the big car and James is waiting outside. We should be home in time for dinner." He turned a beaming face to Doctor Kimberly. "You have done a swell job, Doctor. Name your price and I'll gladly write you a check."

"Take that up with our business manager, Mr. Kent," Bruce said coolly. Somehow this man rubbed him the wrong way.

"What makes you think I'm ready to leave here, Dad?" young Kent demanded.

"Wh-at? What's that?" his father asked, bewildered.

"I'll go home on just one condition, Dad." Rodney explained. "I must have Juliet—my night nurse. She must go with me. I love that girl, Dad, and I'm going to have her, come hell or high water. Wait till you see her. She's everything I ever wanted—all rolled into one perfect woman."

"H'm'm," his father mused. "Where have I heard that before? Don't be absurd, son. You have fancied yourself in love dozens of times and they all petered out, some rather expensively—for me. I don't like mixing business with pleasure, Rod. Forget it. We'll be home in a few hours and——"

"If I go Juliet goes with me," Rodney persisted stubbornly.

The senior Kent shook his head, eying the young man sitting beside the window. "What's her name—Juliet what? Perhaps it can be arranged. We'll see."

"No funny business now, Dad," his son warned. "You do your stuff and it's got to be good, too."

The father turned to encounter the stern, uncompromising face of the Chief-of-Staff. "How about it, Doctor? Can this girl—this Juliet Rod speaks of—go home with us? I'll make it worth your while."

"You couldn't possibly do that," Bruce replied flatly. "Absolutely not. Our nurses do not accompany patients when they leave Kimberly Sanatorium. We cannot spare a single nurse —you should know that. I am afraid your son will have to leave without Miss—the nurse he seems, at the moment, to fancy. That is final."

Mr. Kent looked displeased. "Oh, come now, Doctor," he said in a man-to-man-we-know-you're-just-kidding attitude. "Don't try to tell me that any of your nurses are indispensable. Why, I can send you any number of girls—good ones, too. My son seems to want this particular nurse and I fail to see why he can't have her."

"And I'm telling you that he can't," Bruce told him sharply. "Our nurses are pretty special—trained for our particular type of work, and I must inform you that they are quite indispensable. Your son must become accustomed to another nurse. I would suggest an older woman or perhaps a male nurse. Now if you are quite ready to leave I think we can arrange to have your son discharged within an hour."

"But, my dear Doctor Kimberly——"

"I'm sorry, Mr. Kent," Bruce said stiffly, "I have given you my ultimatum. I'm a busy man with many things to do. When you are ready to leave you may stop at the Business Manager's office—third door on the left from the entrance—where Mr. Allison will take care of you. Good-bye," he said, bowing first to the father and then to his son. "It gives us great satisfaction to feel we have helped restore your son to health, Mr. Kent."

The door closed and father and son stared at each other in something like consternation, but not for long. "You're not going to let him get away with it, are you, Dad?" Rodney exclaimed, angrily. "He can't do this to me. I won't have it. Juliet's my girl—I need her!" He punched his bell and when

Mary Blanchard entered he demanded truculently, "What became of Juliet—go get her."

"Juliet? You mean the night nurse?"

"Of course I mean the night nurse. I know she's off duty, but she isn't dead, is she? Go get her and tell her to get ready to leave this place—at once. Well, don't just stand there. Go——"

"Better do as the boy says, young lady," his father suggested and Mary glared at him.

"Your son isn't running this sanatorium, Mr. Kent," Mary told him grimly. "And we nurses are not servants to do your bidding. We are here to nurse the sick. Oh, I'll go," she muttered, but didn't say where she intended going.

"That's better," the elder Kent soothed. "We don't want any trouble, you know, but my son has been very ill, and what he wants, he gets. I'm sure you understand, Nurse."

"That's what you think," Blanchard said to herself as she left the room. She went directly to the superintendent's office and Miss Kimberly promptly telephoned the nurses' home with orders to refuse admittance to anyone until otherwise notified.

"Lock your doors, Mrs. Davis," she advised the housemother. "I think we have a couple of madmen over here. Oh, not actually, of course, but two of the pampered rich who want to abduct one of our nurses. If you have any trouble, call us back."

And as it happened, Jill Ordway had gone skating with Alan Blake and knew nothing about any trouble at the sanatorium, but Miss Kimberly didn't mention names when she talked with Mrs. Davis. She accompanied Blanchard to Rodney Kent's room where one of the maids was packing his belongings preparatory to his leaving. She motioned the nurse to remain outside and smiled as she entered the room.

"I'm sure you're a happy man, Mr. Kent," she said pleasantly. "I know we are happy for you and thankful your son reacted so well and so promptly to our treatment. I should suggest complete rest and quiet for a few days after you reach home, Rodney. After that, you should be your old self—although a better self, I'm sure. Somehow, there is nothing like a severe illness to discipline one and bring out the innate goodness that is within each one of us. I feel sure you are going to be a better man for this brief intermission. We shall miss you,

129

Rodney. Is there anything you would like before you leave—lunch perhaps—coffee?"

And before Ruth Kimberly's maternal sweetness, neither man dared mention Rodney's demand for Jill's return.

"You have done a grand job here, Miss—er—Kimberly," the elder Kent told her. "We shan't forget. Money can't begin to repay you."

"I'm sure of it, Mr. Kent," the superintendent said smoothly. "Have you everything you need for your journey? Oh, you brought your own car. That's right. I hope your chauffeur wasn't bored waiting outside. He should have come in where it is warm."

"That's all right. He is accustomed to waiting," Mr. Kent told her. "Everything has been arranged for my son's comfort. James understands conditions. He's something of a nurse himself." He laid his arm across his son's broad shoulders and with Doctor Anthony, who had been summoned, on the other side, maneuvered the ex-patient from the room. At the door he halted.

"May I say good-bye to Juliet, Miss Kimberly? I—I don't like leaving without that—after her kindness——"

"I'm afraid that is quite impossible," the superintendent replied. "She is off duty until tomorrow morning and has gone on a trip, I believe. I will give her your message, however. A nurse is always pleased to hear she has been of service."

The little procession moved on to the elevator which deposited them on the main floor. Ruth Kimberly followed. She would be glad to see the last of Rodney Kent—both the Kents, for that matter.

"There is no need of my seeing Allison, Miss—er—Kimberly," Mr. Kent said somewhat sourly. "I have written a check to cover my son's brief stay at the sanatorium. I'm sure you will find it more than generous. I can give it to you and save time. I am in something of a rush to get Rodney home. I'm sure you can appreciate that angle." Ruth glanced at the folded paper he had handed her and gasped indignantly.

"I think you must see our business manager, Mr. Kent," she said sharply. "This way." She knocked on Pete's door, and without waiting for his "come," entered. Mr. Kent was hesitating halfway to the front door. "Pete, come here," she called, and Pete sprang from his chair and joined her. "Mr. Kent wishes to pay his bill. This is Mr. Allison, Mr. Kent. He has your account in readiness for you." She held out the check to him and when he refused to accept it—tore it into four pieces and dropped it on the floor.

"Come inside, Mr. Kent," Pete invited suavely. "Rodney will be quite comfortable where he is for a moment or two. We won't be long." He opened a drawer in his desk and presented an itemized account. The man gasped, sputtered, glowered and flatly refused to pay any such exorbitant sum.

"One thousand dollars for two weeks' treatment! What is this—a gyp?"

Peter Allison smiled. "Are you the man who pleaded and begged Doctor Kimberly to accept your son for treatment—money being no object, just so your son be admitted here? Are you the man who swore you would pay anything—if only Rodney could have his chance? Well, for your edification let me tell you that your son—that precious son of yours—went berserk one night. Broke the arm of the attending physician and beat up his nurse." He reached out and took back the account. "I think, Mr. Kent, our bill is far too small. Perhaps the courts will settle the matter more equitably. Good afternoon. You will hear from us——"

Mr. Kent drew out his checkbook. "How much?" he asked, his voice almost bleating. "We can't have any unfavorable publicity. A thousand, you say?"

"Correct," Peter Allison said coldly. "I am sure it is little enough, Mr. Kent. We have our reputation to maintain, you know. We are glad that your son has recovered, but as you have said repeatedly—impressively—no money can repay Kimberly Sanatorium. It just can't be done. Good afternoon, Mr. Kent. A pleasant journey."

He stood in his office door and watched the departing guests as they left the building. Doctor Anthony joined him and Ruth came from her own office. She had the torn check in her hand. She spread it on his desk and exclaimed:

"One hundred dollars! I was never so insulted in my life," she stormed. "After all we went through with that—that—impossible cad."

Pete whistled softly. "I wish I had hiked it another thousand. Of all the cheapskates! Why, the man has millions and Rodney is his only son, isn't he?"

"Kent?" asked Doctor Anthony, and at the other's nod, went on. "I'll say he has, but he's tighter than a drum and as crooked as they come. His sole object in life is that precious son of his—nothing is too good for Rodney. And I happen to know something about *him*. You're lucky this place is still standing—the fellow's terrific!"

"You're telling us," Pete grinned. "Where's Doc all this time? I thought he was to give Rod the once-over before discharging him. He usually does."

"Oh, he did, all right," Doctor Anthony explained, "and then he went over to the nurses' home. He said something to me about seeing the barn door was locked. I didn't understand what he meant; but he came from Kent's room. I saw him."

Ruth Kimberly laughed softly and Pete Allison frowned. "You know, of course, that Rodney insisted on taking Miss Ordway with him when he left. In fact, he flatly refused to leave without her. His father demanded his son's wishes be granted. Just like that." She laughed again and was surprised to see the look of righteous indignation on Jim Anthony's face.

"The crazy coot!" he muttered. "How dared he even raise his eyes to her? I'd like to punch him right in the nose."

Peter and Ruth exchanged glances. So Jill had another admirer, had she, Ruth told herself. Well, there was safety in numbers. She wondered what Bruce was doing over at the nurses' home and if he had seen Jill.

### 18

THERE FOLLOWED DAYS of hard work and almost unnatural quiet at Kimberly Sanatorium. Spring arrived on laggard feet. Snow and sleet squalls with searching bitter winds made driving hazardous and walking next to impossible. Skating was over for the season, as were bobsledding and skiing. Life seemed drab—spirits low. Not yet did one's blood surge to the call of spring. In fact, it looked as if winter would hang on indefinitely. Sniffles and colds were rampant and Westhaven was full of flu and pneumonia. Hospitals were crowded and doctors and nurses were more than ever overworked.

On this late March morning, Mrs. Botany was moody. Even the branches of forsythia Jill had broken from the giant bush near the garage and brought inside and that now were a mass of pure gold, failed to lift her spirits.

"I feel tragedy in the air, Ruth," she told the superintendent. "Of course you know I am psychic. I *feel* these things," she said solemnly.

"It's the weather, my dear," Miss Kimberly soothed. "I feel sort of edgy myself, but after all, spring is actually here whether we recognize it or not. March is nearly over and with April we shall undoubtedly have better weather with plenty of sunshine. I think it is clearing already. Did I tell you I saw a bluebird yesterday? And robins have been back for weeks. I'm not psychic but you know the old scriptural precept: 'As long as the earth shall stand, seedtime and harvest shall not fail.' It is nearly seedtime, and the old law will hold true. You'll see."

"You and your Scripture!" the old lady sniffed disdainfully. "You've been hobnobbing too much with Bradley upstairs. How long is he going to stay here, anyway? He looks all right —acts all right—chipper and healthy as a lark. Isn't costing *him* anything, I'll wager. His congregation must be crazy. The man's soldiering. I have half a mind to notify them of that fact." She eyed the superintendent slyly to see her reaction to the statement, but Ruth merely smiled.

"Doctor Bradley is a darling, Mrs. Botany. I can't understand why you don't like him."

"You can't, eh? He has my nurse, hasn't he? He's keeping her, too, and he needs a nurse just about as much as a cat needs two tails. Makes me mad. I'm paying as much or more than that benighted congregation of his is paying, or I'll eat a couple of hats—small ones," she grinned elfishly. "I don't think he likes me, Ruth. Hasn't been in to see me in weeks."

"He probably thinks he wouldn't be welcome. The other guests love having him drop in."

"I can't stand psalm-singing, praying hypocrites, Ruth," Mrs. Botany said crossly. "I've more respect for an out-and-out criminal——"

"Listen, you fraud!" Ruth said impulsively. "I'm going to tell Doctor Bradley to come in to see you this very afternoon —for the good of your soul. Dollars to doughnuts you will

133

completely lose your hard old heart to him. But remember, my dear, the man is married and his wife understands him—oh, definitely."

She turned and hurried away, refusing to listen to the sputters of protest from the old lady. She met Jill Ordway returning from the kitchen with her patient's midmorning milk. Jill was looking puzzled. She had an open letter in her hand and held it out to the superintendent.

"This came in the early mail, Ruth," she said, pausing while Miss Kimberly read the few lines. "I can't understand it. I have no relatives that I know of—except my mother. I never knew I had cousins—male or female."

"I shouldn't pay any attention to it," Ruth said. "It is probably the work of some crank or joker. This is your half-day off duty, isn't it? Well, I have an invitation—of sorts—for your patient to call on Mrs. Botany this afternoon if he has nothing better to do. The poor soul is lonely. It's the weather, no doubt, but if anyone can cheer her up it is Doctor Bradley. How we shall miss him when he leaves! Everyone is so fond of him."

Jill retrieved the letter and thrust it into a pocket. It was evident the superintendent thought little of it. "Do you know that I have been frankly puzzled about it, Ruth. Supposing——"

"If the writer is sincere, this Leslie would have come here—not asked you to meet him or her in Westhaven, nor would he have written anything as ambiguous as this. Please don't give it another thought, Jill, and certainly do not keep the date suggested. If it is aboveboard, the writer will call on you here. You are young and attractive, you know, and——"

"All right," the girl said, laughing at the other's gravity. "But I wish people would realize that I was for more than twenty-two months in almost constant danger and survived and that I don't scare easily. What could happen to me in broad daylight, Ruth? Don't be silly."

"Just the same——" Ruth began, then dropped the subject as she saw Jill's annoyance.

Doctor Bradley was quite willing to visit Mrs. Botany, and Ruth left, the contents of Jill's letter fresh in her mind. In Bruce's office a few minutes later, she recounted the incident and saw her brother frown and shake his head.

134

"She isn't going to take any notice of it, I hope," he said.

"I don't know," Ruth murmured. "Jill is very independent, you should remember, and I think she resents any least intimation that she can't take care of herself. I never knew a girl like her. No clinging vine—that one."

"I'll speak to her myself," Bruce said: "This has all the earmarks of a plot—the telephone calls—asking when she was to be free—giving no name—just requesting the information. I don't like it, Ruth. Did you tell her about the calls?" he asked.

Ruth shook her head. "No. I felt it was unnecessary. After all, she is a grown woman, Bruce, and generally Alan, Jeff, or one of the other girls is with her when she goes in to town. You must know there is always something of this sort happening in schools, colleges and hospitals—any institution where there are girls. They are perpetrated by cranks, most of them, or someone with a perverted sense of humor. I simply ignore them."

Bruce sat before his desk staring straight before him, a frown of concentration on his face. "Just the same, I don't like it, Ruth. I have half a mind to turn that letter over to the police. We're somewhat isolated and, after all, these girls are under our care—we're responsible for them—in a measure. Tell Jill I want that letter—or—I'll tell her myself."

"I shouldn't if I were you, darling," his sister advised. "I'm sure she will resent it."

"Let her," the young man muttered as he left the room. Jill and Doctor Bradley were playing chess and Jill was finding the going hard. She rose as the doctor entered the room and he motioned her to be seated. He came to stand behind her chair and she was annoyed to feel her nerves quiver at his nearness.

"Just in time to watch me win a tremendous victory, Doctor," the clergyman said, leaning back in his chair and enjoying the rich color that ebbed and flowed in Jill's lovely face. "Or have you something on your mind?"

"May I borrow your nurse for a moment, Doctor?" he asked and at the other's permission, went on, "There is something I want to discuss with you, Ordway, if you will come with me." Puzzled, the girl joined him in the corridor outside and stood while he continued, "My sister has told me about your receiving an anonymous letter this morning. Oh, I know it was

135

signed 'Leslie,' which probably means absolutely nothing. She said you were at a loss concerning the author. Will you let me have that letter, Jill? I am interested in tracing it. It looks quite fishy to me."

Jill stiffened. "I'm sure it need not concern you in the least, Doctor Kimberly," she said coolly.

Bruce frowned. "Surely you aren't contemplating——"

"I haven't decided what I shall do—yet," Jill said.

"And you refuse to give me the letter? Don't be difficult, Jill," he went on placatingly. "After all, we are responsible——"

"Nonsense!" the girl interrupted shortly. "We are women here—trained nurses—not morons, Doctor Kimberly," she said sharply. "And I, for one, dislike being treated as such. Is that all?"

"What ails you, Jill?" the exasperated young man asked. "You used to be——"

"Forget it!" Jill interrupted again and left him. Both were fuming and the girl wondered that she dared treat the Chief-of-staff so summarily, but she was angry. Doctor Kimberly walked away.

"Somehow I never thought Jill was obstinate or pig-headed," he said to himself as he went back to his office. "She used to listen to me—take my advice—treat me with respect!"

His office was empty when he returned to it and he sank back in his chair and stared unseeing at the bleak landscape. No doubt Jill's changed attitude was due to her association with Alan Blake. Probably she was in love with the fellow. He got up and strode to the window. A smart green convertible was passing—dawdling—the driver peering out at the sprawling sanatorium. Bruce watched and saw the car turn in front of the nurses' home and come slowly back. He remained at the window for several minutes while the same car passed and re-passed, the driver apparently more than usually interested in the building. Suddenly he went into the hall, donned his overcoat and slipped out to the gate. The wind was bitter and he found shelter behind a giant elm. There it came again—the same car. Now what did the fellow want? As it came abreast of him Bruce caught his breath for a moment. It was—it certainly was Rodney Kent. So he hadn't given up the idea of taking Jill away. No doubt it was he who had written that note

136

and he who had been telephoning so persistently. Bruce felt a wild desire to throttle that brash young man—to teach him a sound lesson. But how? He would get little or no assistance from Jill—that he knew. He remained standing behind the tree for some time longer, but evidently the driver was satisfied for the time being and had gone on to Westhaven.

Bruce returned to the warmth of his own office but he was deeply concerned. Ruth had told him that Jill was free for the afternoon and evening—free to fall into the trap young Kent had so cleverly laid. He paced the floor uncertain what to do. He knew Jill was angry with him and would resent any further mention of the letter—no doubt she would also resent it if he mentioned seeing Rodney Kent patrolling the place. He swore softly to himself, then snapped his fingers as a sudden idea came to him.

"I'll do it!" he muttered, and dialed the number of the most exclusive night club in Meredith, making reservations for the evening. Then he called Jeff Thomas into his office and practically demanded that he invite Jill to spend the afternoon and evening with him. Jeff demurred. He was just about sold on the idea of an evening's work at the laboratory. Why didn't Doc go himself—it would do him good—get him out of the rut he seemed to have fallen into. But, of course, Bruce knew Jill would refuse any invitation from him for this evening. Jeff must act as his ambassador. As Jeff continued to demur, Bruce unburdened himself and Doctor Thomas whistled.

"Is this rural Westhaven?" he wanted to know. "Is this the twentieth century and are we talking about Juliet Ordway, erstwhile Army nurse with the rank of Lieutenant? You've gone nuts, Doc. What on earth could Kent do—in broad daylight? Seems to me you're not paying a very great compliment to the lady. What do you suppose she would be doing all the time Rodney was planning this abduction—if any? She's a good strong gal, Doc, and nobody's fool. Forget the meller-drammer, old man, and rest your imagination." He sounded bored.

"You're no help to me, Jeff Thomas," Bruce complained. "I tell you this is serious. I feel it. The boy has a bad reputation. His father will stop at nothing to give his son the thing he wants. I don't like it."

"So you don't like it? Why don't you marry the gal, Doc?"

137

he demanded. "You act like a lovesick adolescent afraid the big bad wolf will carry off your frail sweetheart. Rot!"

"Thanks for nothing," Bruce said coldly. "Okay, okay, so you won't take any of it seriously. That's all, Doctor Thomas. You may return to your laboratory and the experiments that are so important." He turned away and Jeff sidled toward the door. He was grinning as he went out, but sobered when he reached his own domain. He recalled the gorillalike strength of young Kent and the ease with which he had disabled both Doctor Judson and Jill Ordway. Maybe he could influence Jill—or get Ann to do it. He went in search of Ann Burke. But Ann was nowhere to be found and Jill seemed inaccessible. All right, he would ask Jill for a date. He would do more than that for a pal. He accosted Jill as she went off duty at noon. She was on her way to the dining room.

"Hi!" he greeted her, a restraining hand on her arm. "How's about giving me a break this P.M., dolling? I have a yen to drive over to Meredith and inspect the new wing on Hope General Hospital. We could have dinner at the Casino and maybe dance some or see a show. How about it, beautiful? Can do?"

"I'm sorry, Jeff," Jill told him and meant it. She liked this glib young doctor and always enjoyed a date with him. "I half promised Alan I would save the afternoon and evening for him. What's the matter? Ann on duty?"

"As a matter of fact, she is; but that isn't the reason I asked you. We haven't been seeing very much of each other lately and—well—I'm extremely fond of you, Juliet. What are you and Blake planning on doing—as if it was any of my business?"

"Oh," Jill shrugged, "nothing much. Maybe drive out to his place or a movie, perhaps. It is never necessary to plan with Alan, you know. He can always make a date interesting."

"I see," Jeff murmured. "Well, just so long as you keep out of mischief it's okay by me, dolling. S'long—have fun."

And Jill went on down to dinner. She had forgotten for the time being her argument and subsequent anger with Doctor Kimberly. In fact, she had even forgotten its cause. She had no intention of keeping an engagement with a phantom cousin. If Alan Blake came, she would probably spend a pleasant time with him but she felt at the present moment

138

she didn't care if he came or not. She finished dinner and went on to the nurses' home where she attended to the hundred and one things a girl finds to do when she is away from home. It was only a little after two when Alan telephoned to tell of an important business engagement he and his father had for the afternoon but he hoped to be back by eight and would drive in and they might have dinner some place and dance. Jill told him that was all right with her and went on pressing one of her frocks.

The day had brightened considerably. The wind died to a low murmur. The sun made brief snatches at the gloom until by four the clouds fled and the sky turned an amazing blue. Why, the ground was almost dry. What a day for a walk along the quiet country roads! Jill slipped on heavy walking shoes, donned a wool skirt and short fur jacket, settled a brown beret firmly on her bright head and sallied forth. This was just what she needed. She had been cooped up too long. She met but few cars—a bus lumbered past and a truck halted to offer her a lift. But she shook her head and went on. She was a good walker and she had traveled much farther than she realized, when a green convertible passed, stopped and waited until she came abreast.

"Hi, Juliet!" someone called, and she turned in amazement to meet the knowing gaze of Rodney Kent. He opened the car door invitingly. "Hop in, beautiful—let's go places."

Jill shook her head and turned to retrace her steps. "Hello, Rodney," she said coolly. "I'm out for exercise. How are you? You look on top of the world. I'm glad. Nice to have seen you again." She lifted a hand in salute and farewell and started back toward the sanatorium. The young man didn't move for a moment, then he drew up to one side of the road and got out.

"Here, what's your hurry?" he asked as he reached her side. His voice was filled with laughter. This was fun. "When I invite a gal to hop in, I expect her to do just that. Come on now, Juliet, give me a break. The old saw-bones back there thought he had put one over on me, but he didn't know Rodney Kent." His arm encircled her slim waist and he drew her close, pinning her arms against him. "I'm strong—very strong, baby. Better come peaceably. What I want I take. That's my motto."

His free hand came down against her mouth and he lifted her easily and carried her to his car where he set her down while he opened the door. "Hop in, Juliet," he ordered. "What are you afraid of—Big Chief Kimberly back there? I'll take care of you, baby—don't you ever forget that. Comfy?" he asked as he set the car in motion. "I could tie you in if I thought it necessary, but I'm sure it won't be. Gals all like strong men—dominant males, you know. They all fall for it —even you."

He laughed gleefully and Jill thought she detected an insane note in that laughter. But she gave no sign of fear. She sank back against the soft leather upholstery and tried to relax. This was the twentieth century—broad daylight and she was a trained nurse having overseas experience. This untamed youngster beside her was fancying himself in the role of cave man. She would pretend to fall in with his plan—provided it didn't last too long or demand too much of her.

They passed through the small settlement occupied by the Blake family and its employees and on toward Meredith where she knew she had only to scream to bring help, but she didn't want a scene. After all, she had the sanatorium to consider. As that idea came to her she recalled her conversation with Bruce Kimberly that morning. Why had he been so hateful? Why had she resented his concern for her safety? He evidentl' knew more about Rodney Kent than she did.

"Why so silent, baby?" Rodney asked, slowing his break neck speed somewhat as they approached a hairpin curve.

"What is there to say?" Jill asked coolly in her turn.

"Plenty, sweetheart. Oh—oh! Close shave that time, bu don't you worry. I'm a swell driver—none better. You ought to have been along in some of the tight places I've squeezed out of. Nothing to it. Just nerve and a good strong right. That does it every time. Gosh, you roadhog!" he screamed suddenly. "Move over! Move over!" The driver of the loaded truck appeared deaf to the demand. Rodney screamed again. "Move over! If you don't I'll—I'll make you—you—uh—er —sorry, baby, but I'll teach that bird a lesson——"

Followed a deafening crash—an unearthly scream of teror and merciful oblivion gathered Jill into its comforting folds.

Jill knew little or nothing of what followed. And it was

hours later that she opened her eyes in a strange room. A light burned softly on a table not far away and a girl in nurse's uniform looked up at her faint exclamation. Jill had tried to sit up and groaned as innumerable pains shot through her body and she promptly lost consciousness. But it didn't last long this time and she roused to find the nurse standing beside the bed with an elderly man in hospital whites close by. They smiled encouragement at her look of bewilderment.

"Take it easy," the doctor told her.

"Wh-where—am—I? Wh-at—hap-happened?" she whispered.

"There was an accident," the doctor explained casually. "You are in Hope General Hospital in Meredith."

"The—new—wing, Jeff?"

The nurse looked puzzled, but the doctor went on as if she had not spoken. "You are more bruised than broken, young lady," he said kindly. "Your companion didn't escape so easily. Can you tell us your name and your address? We should get word to your people, who are probably very much concerned."

"People?" the girl asked. Then with an effort she seemed to collect her scattered memory. "Jill—Jill Ordway," she said haltingly. "Tell him I'm sorry." She shook her head and winced, then went on. "Kimberly Sanatorium. I'm a nurse. Doctor Kimberly——" She was seized with uncontrollable shivering and once again she fainted. She struggled up from the vast blackness at last and opened her eyes to find Doctor Kimberly sitting beside the bed, his fingers on her pulse.

She stared at him for a moment, eyes widening—a shining glory in them that brought the man beside her to his knees. But the gray eyes closed and she turned her face to the wall, a whimper of pain escaping her lips.

"Darling—darling!" Bruce breathed. He pressed her lax hand to his lips. "Thank God, you are all right!"

"No," she denied childishly. "I hurt. I hurt a ver."

"I know, sweetheart, but you will soon be w    —now that I have you back—my old darling Jill!"

The bright head turned to him. She examined face with something like wonder for a long moment, the   e sm    wr ly. "Hello, Kim!" she murmured. "I—guess—I      —as smart—as I—th-thought—I was."

He pressed her hand in his, his voice was ragged. "Why

141

did you go with him, Jill? After what you knew about him —what he did to you and Judson?"

"Ouch!" the girl cried, wincing as she moved experimentally. Her head shifted from side to side in an effort to rid it of the feeling of inadequacy. "I had no choice. He's a very strong man, Kim," she explained, frowning. "Is he hurt—badly?"

"Not nearly as badly as he deserved," Bruce told her grimly. "He might have killed you. It's a miracle he didn't. The crazy fool!"

"But——" began Jill.

"He doesn't merit your concern, darling. One of his hips is broken, a couple of ribs and a shoulder. I believe there was some concussion as well. He will be laid up for a long time, and have plenty of leisure in which to repent. And I hope——"

"Don't say it—please!" the girl begged. "I know it serves me right for being so stubborn and know-it-all, but I never once dreamed of anyone trying to kidnap me—me—Jill Ordway, late of the U. S. Army Nurses' Corps. I think I can believe anything possible after this. When can I go home, Kim?"

"In a day or two, perhaps. I wish I could take you right now, darling. Ruth is beside herself and the rest of the staff are ready to commit mayhem or possibly even murder. I think I never in my whole life saw a group of people quite so angry as the staff of Kimberly Sanatorium—and the few patients interested—when news came bringing details of your plight. You are very dear to us all, darling."

Jill's eyes filled with tears. "I was a silly fool to ignore your warning, Kim," she said humbly. "Give them all my love and tell them I hope to be back very soon."

She was very tired—everything seemed vague—unreal. Even Kim was a product of her imagination. Wasn't he madly in love with Sylvia Webster? Of course. She must remember this was all just a dream—but such a lovely dream. Her eyelids drooped even while Bruce lingered for a few last instructions to the attending nurse. It was, of course, just a continuation of her Kim bent over her and pressed his lips against she sighed and smiled in her sleep.

## 19

JILL'S RECOVERY WAS rapid and within a few days she was back at the nurses' home receiving congratulations as well as innumerable questions from the curious. She had little to tell. Everything had happened so quickly. She was annoyed that the affair had reached the newspapers. The sanatorium had tried to make light of it but the name of Rodney Kent meant news and reporters had rushed to interview Bruce and Pete with but slim results. At the Hope General Hospital in Meredith, Jill had been protected but Rodney seemed to welcome visitors, his father, who had hastened to his bedside, notwithstanding. The elder Kent was extremely bitter toward Jill—blaming her for his son's mad infatuation—and Jill was glad to leave for Westhaven and the quiet seclusion of the nurses' home. She expected to return to duty within a few days. She considered her position as Doctor Bradley's nurse something of a sinecure but she knew he missed her.

Doctor Kimberly had been to see her every day during her stay in the Meredith hospital and Jill appeared to have completely forgotten everything about that first visit. She was cool and matter-of-fact in the extreme and the young man was puzzled. What had happened to change her? Of course Pete and Ruth had called, bringing quantities of spring blossoms, and Jeff Thomas and Ann Burke had spent a couple of hours with her, as had Alan Blake. Alan was for finishing the job on young Kent that his ungovernable temper had muffed. He wanted to take Jill home to his mother for a long convalescence. To his chagrin, Jill laughed at him.

"I'm all right, Alan," she assured him. "Don't be silly." She was relieved when Bruce arrived, and Alan departed in something of a huff. It was the first time she had felt at all nervous in Alan's company. She hoped he wasn't going to spoil things for them both by asking her to marry him. She didn't want to marry anyone. She wanted to go back to work. She felt sure a great many things had happened while she was away, although Ruth and Ann had assured her the place had been like a morgue without her.

"Mr. Kent paid us a visit early this morning, Ruth," Peter Allison said later in the day as he paced his chief's office. "Imagine! Wanted to know what we intended doing about his son's accident. He informed me the car was fully insured and the company would pay any reasonable amount Miss Ordway should demand."

"I felt like kicking the old shyster into the middle of next week," Bruce added vindictively. "He polluted the very air we have to breathe here."

"What did you decide to do?" Ruth wanted to know. "Jill certainly is entitled to something in the way of compensation for all she has endured from that—that——"

Pete laughed and laid restraining fingers against her lips. "Don't get all het up over it, darling," he soothed. "He isn't worth it."

"But what did you tell him?"

"I told him to take his money and get out and to keep that son of his away from here or it would cost him plenty."

"Yes," Bruce added, "and you should have seen the look of astonishment and disbelief on the old codger's face when he realized we weren't going to gouge him. How is Jill feeling, Ruth?" he asked.

Ruth laughed at him. "You saw her yourself not an hour ago," she reminded him. "She'll be all right. Jill's a fine strong girl. I'm glad she's back. We couldn't spare her."

Ruth and Pete drifted away. "Have dinner with me tonight, Ruth," Pete pleaded. "You manage to crawl out of every date I make with you. Tell me, is it that you don't like going out with me?"

Ruth shook her head. "Don't be silly. But you must know I'm a busy woman——"

"Just as I'm a busy man. Listen, Miss Kimberly, will it be news to you if I tell you that I love you? That I want you to be my wife?"

Ruth stared at him for a moment, her face alternately flushing and paling. "I—I—don't know what to say, Pete," she stammered at last. "Are you sure?"

"As I live and breathe. What do you say? Will you marry me?" His voice sank to an impassioned whisper. "Can you love me, dearest?" He was very close there in the wide front hall which, fortunately, at the moment, was empty.

Ruth Kimberly's face was suddenly radiant. She smiled into the eyes searching her own and held out her hands. "If you want me," she said sweetly. "I can think of nothing more wonderful than to be your wife." And ignoring the fact that anyone or everyone might witness the scene, Peter Allison, Kimberly Sanatorium's business manager, took the superintendent of nurses into his arms. It was an exaggerated "ahem!" from Bruce that made them draw apart. Pete kept a firm hold of Ruth's hand, however, as he led her to her brother.

"Will you trust her to me, Bruce? Say you will. I know I am asking a great deal but—she's my girl, Doc, and I'm her man."

Bruce laughed somewhat shakily. He raised his hands above their heads and said solemnly but with deep sincerity, "Bless you, my dear children! There is no one else to whom I could so willingly give this beloved sister of mine, Pete." He kissed Ruth's glowing cheek and shook hands vigorously with his business manager. "I wasn't exactly bowled over by this, you know. I seem to have noticed the symptoms at various times."

"I think we have been very discreet, Bruce," Ruth said, hurrying off on her daily affairs, but she was ecstatically happy. She knew Pete was watching and turned at the top of the stairs to blow him a kiss, but as he started to mount to her she fled. It was all so beautifully new and strange yet.

Bruce returned to his office. He was happy for his beloved sister who all her life had been so much to him, and yet he experienced a feeling almost of depression. Life would be very drab without Ruth. But she had a right to a life of her own—home, husband and children. No, he couldn't begrudge them to her. He walked to the window overlooking the spacious sanatorium grounds. Almost overnight the place had taken on an air of joyous awakening. Crocuses—pink, orchid, yellow and white, spread like a variegated carpet as far as the eye could see. There must have been millions of them. The hedges and shrubbery were showing a fuzz of soft green. Spikes of tulips and daffodils pushed their way through the covering of leaves. Robins poked about in the grass or sang from the top of the tallest tree. And over all, the sun shone gloriously. He felt an urge to visit the brook that ran nosily through the tiny grove and down the hill to the lake a mile away. He looked at his desk. It wasn't too cluttered. Everyone in the

145

sanatorium was progressing nicely. He felt like playing hookey and, by jingo! that's just what he was going to do.

Almost stealthily and with a feeling of guilt which he thrust determinedly behind him, Doctor Kimberly slipped out the side door, along the narrow flag walk, through the hedge and down the hill to the grove. He felt the sun warm on his bare head and his spirits lifted. He heard the chattering of the busy little stream before he could see it, and quickened his pace. How good it all smelled. A splash of scarlet caught his eye and he drew in his breath. That was the lining of a nurse's cape. Somehow he knew it belonged to one nurse in particular, although he couldn't have told why.

Jill had thrown back her cape and was crouched before a great bed of violets—purple and white. She was busily picking them, quite unaware of Bruce's presence, and suddenly he felt like a trespasser.

"M'm'm!" the girl murmured as she held a fragrant bouquet to her face. "And trilliums, too!" she exclaimed aloud. "I must have some." She moved on among the trees and again went down on her knees in the midst of this fresh discovery. Bruce remained standing, his eyes devouring the lovely picture. Then a cry of dismay startled him and he hurried forward.

"What is it?" he asked, reaching her side.

Jill shuddered. "A snake—see? Oh-oo! I detest the slimy creatures." She turned her back and shuddered. Bruce laughed.

"Not scared?" he teased.

"No-o, just—well—sort of disgusted. They're so slimy—so repulsive. I have never been able to overcome the loathing they rouse in me. Aren't you going to kill it?" she demanded as she shudderingly watched the reptile slither through the leaves.

"Of course not," the doctor replied. "It is quite harmless and probably is very useful. Even snakes and worms have their uses, Jill."

"That has all the earmarks of double talk, Doctor," Jill said ruefully.

Bruce laughed. "The farthest thing from my mind," he told her. "I leave that sort of thing to Jeff and Pete. They are experts at it. How are you feeling?"

"Still fine," the girl smiled. "And I expect to go back to

146

work tomorrow. It does seem as if I have been off duty a great deal lately, doesn't it?" She started to walk back to the nurses' home and Bruce laid a restraining hand on her arm.

"Don't go just yet, Jill," he begged. "I want to talk to you. What has changed you? We used to have fun together——"

"I haven't changed, Doctor," Jill said, wishing she were somewhere else. "I must put these flowers in water. See, they are beginning to wilt already."

"You avoid me—ignore my advice——"

"Please don't rub it in, Doctor," she interrupted ruefully. "I have explained all I understood about that affair——"

"Explained, yes," Bruce said raggedly. "Do you know that I nearly lost my mind from worry the afternoon you disappeared? Oh, Jill, Jill—don't you understand? Can't you see how it is with me?"

The girl raised startled eyes to his face. "I—I don't understand. What about Syl—Miss Webster?"

"That has been over for some time, Jill. It should have ended long ago—before ever I returned home. I—we tried to patch things up—tried to revive a dead infatuation but it didn't work. You used to like me in the old days, Jill. Do you remember——"

"Don't!" Jill said sharply. "It can't be—you were so very much in love. I must go back, Doctor Kimberly. Please try to understand. Love isn't something one can put on and take off like an unbecoming or outworn garment. It goes deeper— into the very core of one's being—till death and after."

"Wait!" the young man urged. "I don't want to hurry you —just let us be friends—as we used to be. Perhaps I have been too precipitate, but you see," he smiled into her troubled face, "Ruth and Pete Allison are going to be married and I suppose it is sort of in the air. You must know I'm fond of you, Jill—more than fond, but we'll let it go at that for the time being. Just give me a break—let us be as we once were."

"I'm so glad for them," Jill said enthusiastically, ignoring the last. "Do you know, I have suspected something of the sort. I adore Ruth and I think Mr. Allison is splendid. Is it a secret or may I give Ruth my best wishes?"

"By all means," Bruce told her. "I think the crucial point was reached this morning right outside my office door in the entrance hall, in plain sight and sound of the public—

147

if any. I imagine, however, it would have made little difference to them. They have lived in a world of their own for weeks now. I was amused at their air of springing a surprise on me. But I guess love is like that, isn't it?"

"You should be a better judge of that than I, Doctor," Jill murmured, and hastened her steps.

"Will you have dinner with me tonight, Jill, and if you are well enough we might dance for a while or see a picture? How about it? You have dates with everyone else, why not with me? We used to have fun together. Remember? Please, Jill," he entreated.

"Don't ever be humble, Bruce Kimberly," Jill said unexpectedly. "It doesn't become you."

"All right," the man said resolutely. "I shall call for you at seven-thirty tonight and please be ready. I dislike waiting—as you very well know. All right. Run along and don't forget we have a date, young lady."

Jill ran along the path, then stopped abruptly. "It isn't ethical for a nurse to have social relations with the Chief-of-Staff, Doctor," she called back to him. "It just isn't done."

"Wait and see!" Bruce shouted. "I'll be there."

He returned to his office feeling like a two-year-old. It was a grand world—a grand life! He sat down at his desk and somehow the pile of correspondence quickly shrank to negligible proportions. There would be little for Ruth to do later.

"So you're going out with the boss?" Ann said as she dropped down on Jill's bed that evening. "How very improper!"

Jill turned on her indignantly. "Don't be like that, Ann," she cried. "It's only because he feels he owes me something because of all I have been through. After all—— Oh, skip it!"

"More power to you, darling," her friend soothed. "Now I have hopes for the big lug. Jeff says he is beginning to wake up. The boy friend is tickled pink, just in case you're interested, and sent his blessing."

"For Heaven's sake, Ann," Jill exclaimed in exasperation. "One date doesn't mean marriage or even an engagement any more than one robin means spring."

"No!" Ann said derisively, "but you'll notice that nine

148

times out of ten it does—I mean the robin part of it. I wonder if you'll run into your predecessor, darling. If you do,
how will you act? It might prove embarrassing—or will it?"

"I do think you have the strangest ideas, Ann Burke," Jill
told her a bit shortly. "We're probably going to Meredith
and will see no one either of us knows."

"Well, you look divine, Juliet, and I hope if you do meet
the fair Sylvia that you knock her dead. I'd sure like to be a
mouse and watch."

"You should be a scenario writer, Ann," Jill said derisively,
lifting her wrap from the chair where she had hung it. "I
think you missed your calling." She glanced at the time. "He
should be here. Seven-thirty."

Ann giggled. " 'Oh, Romeo, Romeo! Wherefore art thou,
Romeo?' "

"Shut up!" Jill cried, flushing. "Oh, there's the bell. Be
seeing you."

Jill's knees were trembling as she went down the stairs to
meet Bruce and she chided herself for being silly. His eyes
told her she was lovely and he settled her in his car almost
tenderly, carefully protecting her skirts from contact with
fender and door. The spring night was mild and all the odors
of wood and field swept through the open windows of the
car. Jill felt her taunt nerves relax and she sighed in pleasure.

"Have you ever been to the Casino in Meredith, Jill?"
Bruce asked as they approached the neighboring town. "Some
day I shall tell you a story about it that will probably amuse
you."

"But not now?" Jill asked for something to say.

"Not now, at least not just now. Maybe later. We'll see."

And as they found their table in the fashionable night club,
she wondered what the story might be. The place was crowded
and she looked about curiously. She knew no one. People spoke
to Bruce and looked her over with interest and some curiosity.
And then the unexpected happened. Sylvia Webster entered
with a party of seven and as they followed the waiter to their
table, Sylvia spotted Bruce. With a little cry of delight she left
her friends and hurried over to him, her hands outstretched.
Jill watched his face. How would he greet his former sweetheart? It would tell her what she wanted to know. He rose
and took the newcomer's hands in his.

149

"Greetings, Sylvia!" he said cordially and Jill let out the breath she had been unconsciously holding. Bruce was right— anything he had once felt for Sylvia Webster was dead— definitely and finally.

Miss Webster's eyes swept over the other occupant of Bruce's table and the expression on her face subtly altered. She thrust out one hand and for a moment Jill wondered if she was about to be slapped, then Sylvia laughed, almost mockingly.

"Darling!" she cried, shaking a slim finger at Bruce, "what mischief have you been getting into while I have been gone? Oh! I do remember now. It's your nurse—why—how do you do, Miss—er——" She laughed again and murmured, "I can't remember your name but it doesn't really matter, does it?"

"Not at all," Jill replied sweetly, "since I am changing it so soon."

Now what on earth made me say that, Jill asked herself. I had better wait until I'm asked. But from the look on Bruce's face she knew she hadn't long to wait.

"How thrilling!" Sylvia purred after a rather long moment. "I suspected something of the sort—oh, ages ago—when you first came to Westhaven. Congratulations, Miss—er—— It doesn't matter." She turned, still smiling, and joined her party at a table across the room.

"You meant it, darling, didn't you?" Bruce asked softly when they were alone.

"Yes," Jill told him simply. "I suddenly seemed to know."

"When?"

"Whenever you like, Kim," she answered.

"Let's get out of here," the man said urgently. "I'm not in the least hungry—for food. Are you?"

Jill shook her head and he reached for her wrap. The waiter came, bringing their dinner. Bruce handed him a bill with a whispered explanation—of sorts, and hurried Jill from the room. In the warm spring darkness he took her in his arms and the poignant memory of the months of unhappiness and long-ing fell away from the girl's heart. This was what she had dreamed of—this was why she was born.

It was late when they returned to the sanatorium and seeing a light in the living room of his home, Bruce urged Jill to come in with him and tell his sister the great news. Pete Allison was just leaving. He stood with Ruth in the dim hall and

150

grinned as Bruce and Jill came in. Ruth extended a folded paper to her brother before he could say anything.

"You're just in time to witness a very important ceremony, Bruce," she said. "Come inside—all of you." She touched a match to the wood in the grate then turned to announce in a voice vibrant with happy excitement, "This is the mortgage—tonight we burn it! Kimberly Sanatorium is ours, Bruce, free and clear!"

Bruce snatched the charred paper from the fire. "What is this, Ruth?" he demanded.

"Why, it's the mortage," his sister replied. "Pete's engagement present."

"I won't have it," Bruce said stiffly. "We pay our debts, Allison. And how is it you have it to give away?"

"I bought up the mortgage, fella, when I fell in love with Ruth. Everything I have or hope to have is hers, Doc. Don't begrudge her the pleasure of being generous. And for Heaven's sake, don't go noble on us. I'm soon to be in the family and—— Sa-ay! What goes on here? What have you two been up to? Do you see what I see, darling?" he asked his fiancée.

Ruth laughed and hugged Jill. "I see that at long last these two have come to their senses. Now we shall surely make Kimberly Sanatorium the success we dreamed of. I am so happy for you, my dear," she said as she kissed her brother. "It is what I have hoped and prayed would happen." She retrieved the mortgage papers from her brother's still reluctant fingers and once again tossed them into the fire. This time they vanished into thin gray smoke and she sighed contentedly.

"I could stand a cup of coffee, darling," Pete said in a stage whisper. "Do you have anything of the sort handy or must I raid a wagon back in town? I suppose you two," indicating the newcomers, "have dined sumptuously and aren't interested."

Bruce laughed. "To tell you the truth, Pete, we left without touching a thing. We had more important business at the moment. Come on, sweet, let's eat."

The four trooped off to the kitchen in search of food, for even lovers must eat.